# NEVER LET ME GO

It was love at first sight for Nurse Chloe Perle and ambitious Dr. Adam Raven, but their employer had plans for his daughter, Susannah, and the young doctor. When Adam informed Chloe his career would always come before romantic entanglements, she left the practice for a position far away in the Cotswolds. There, she attracted the attention of Benedict, a handsome young artist. Afraid that he had lost Chloe forever, Adam begged her friend, Betty, the only person who knew her whereabouts, to help him.

*Books by Toni Anders*
*in the Linford Romance Library:*

A LETTER TO MY LOVE
DANCE IN MY HEART
RIVALS IN LOVE

TONI ANDERS

# NEVER LET ME GO

*Complete and Unabridged*

## LINFORD
*Leicester*

First published in Great Britain in 2007

First Linford Edition
published 2008

British Library CIP Data

Anders, Toni
Never let me go.—Large print ed.—
Linford romance library
1. Nurse and physician—Fiction
2. Love stories
3. Large type books
I. Title
823.9'2 [F]

ISBN 978-1-84782-294-9

Published by
F. A. Thorpe (Publishing)
Anstey, Leicestershire

Set by Words & Graphics Ltd.
Anstey, Leicestershire
Printed and bound in Great Britain by
T. J. International Ltd., Padstow, Cornwall

This book is printed on acid-free paper

# Summer, 1926

Betty brought her bicycle to a halt outside a large Victorian house and after climbing down from the saddle, began to wheel her bike up the drive.

'We're here,' she called to her friend, Chloe, who was cycling behind.

Chloe also dismounted, but stopped to read the brass plaque on the gatepost. *Dr Arthur Blaine MD*, it said in large letters. Then underneath in smaller script was engraved, *Dr Gordon Ramsden MD*, and beneath that, *Dr Adam Raven MD*.

'This way,' called Betty, wheeling her bike round to the back of the house where she leaned it against the wall, underneath a wooden shelter.

Chloe followed suit and the two girls entered the building through a side door.

'I'll take you to Dr Blaine first, and

1

then I must go and prepare the treatment room — he'll introduce you to everyone else,' said Betty.

They walked down a black and white tiled corridor to a square hallway and Betty knocked on one of the heavy oak doors.

'Come in,' called a deep voice.

Betty gave her friend a reassuring smile and opened the door.

'Here is Nurse Perle, Dr Blaine.'

Betty stood aside as Chloe entered the room, and closed the door behind her.

Dr Blaine continued writing at his desk for a few seconds, then looked up.

'Nurse Perle? Good morning. Please sit down.'

He gestured towards a chair.

Chloe sat down and waited. She had been interviewed for the post of nurse at the surgery two weeks ago and had found Dr Blaine rather alarming at the time. She felt no happier about him now, but she had liked the sound of the job and was determined to do well at it.

'You are a friend of Nurse Wilson?'

'Yes. We trained together. I'm lodging with her at her aunt's house.'

'Good. Good. She can instruct you on how we like things done in this practice.'

He took his watch from his waistcoat pocket and peered at it.

'I can spare a quarter of an hour to show you around. Come along. Come along.'

He led the way from the surgery, and Chloe hurried to keep up with him as he charged along the corridor to open the door of the room next to his own.

'My secretary, Miss Garland. Miss Garland, this is Nurse Chloe Perle, our new nurse.' He introduced a small mousy woman with an Eton crop who was typing at a heavy typewriter.

Miss Garland bobbed up nervously and Chloe shook her hand hurriedly before Dr Blaine led her away to the next room.

He knocked and opened the door and Dr Gordon Ramsden rose to his feet behind his desk. He was tall and thin with fiery red hair.

'We're glad to have another nurse,' he said, shaking Chloe's hand after Dr Blaine had introduced her. 'There's too much for Nurse Wilson to do alone.'

The next room was the waiting area where a pleasant-faced woman of about forty sat behind a desk.

'Miss Jenkins, our receptionist,' announced Dr Blaine and Chloe shook hands with yet another new colleague.

Chloe hoped she would remember all these names and went through them in her mind. Dr Blaine, Dr Ramsden, Miss Garland, Miss Jenkins — surely there was someone else. Wasn't there another doctor working at the practice?

As they crossed the hall, the front door opened and a tall, handsome man stood on the threshold.

'Dr Raven,' the older man called out in greeting. 'Come and meet our new nurse.'

Dr Raven took a few steps into the hall before stopping abruptly to stand gazing intently at Chloe.

An avid reader of romantic novels, Chloe could hum all the latest love songs. She regularly visited the picture-house so she knew all about love at first sight but had always thought it a silly notion.

Now, suddenly and unexpectedly, she wondered if such a thing could be possible after all.

To her, it seemed that she and Dr Raven stood and stared at each other for hours, but it was really only for a moment. She took in the thick brown hair and the green eyes under heavy brows.

'Nurse Perle. Welcome.'

His voice was low and expressive. His hand held hers longer than was necessary but she could not pull away.

Dr Blaine seemed not to have noticed their reaction to each other.

'Come along, Nurse Perle,' he said, hurrying her away and down a side passage. 'I'll take you to Nurse Wilson and she can get you started. Come to me if you have any problems.'

He opened a door and, still in a daze, Chloe found herself alone in the treatment room.

There was a small mirror on the wall and she studied her reflection with interest. But she looked the same as usual: pale face, pale hair — nothing to show that she had just fallen madly in love with a complete stranger!

She sat down on the end of the treatment bed.

Her life had changed! Nothing would be the same again!

Then the door opened and Betty came in, changed into her nurse's white dress and crisply starched cap.

'There you are! Did you meet everyone? Your uniform is here. Change in the little cloakroom in the corner. But hurry. The first patient will be here in a few minutes.'

★　★　★

They were so busy that the morning went by in a flash.

She had to learn routines and study timetables, find out where everything was kept and assist Betty with a variety of patients. Before she realised it, it was one o'clock.

'We eat lunch in the garden if the weather is fine,' said Betty, giving her hands a thorough wash and picking up her bag.

Chloe did the same and the two of them went out into the garden by the same side door that they'd used when they'd arrived that morning.

Outside, wooden chairs and benches were arranged around a table that had been placed beneath a shady tree and once the girls had settled themselves they took out the packets of sandwiches that had been prepared for them by Betty's Aunt Ellen.

They were soon joined by Miss Garland and Miss Jenkins, the latter carrying a tray of tea which she placed on the table.

'We take it in turns to make the tea,' explained Miss Garland, pouring each girl a cup. 'It will be your turn on Thursday, Chloe.'

They all ate in shy silence for a while, then Miss Jenkins broke the ice by asking whether Chloe thought she would like working at the surgery.

'Oh, I'm sure I shall,' answered Chloe enthusiastically. 'Everyone seems so nice.'

After that everyone chattered happily about nothing in particular until it was time to go back to work.

'Where do the doctors eat?' Chloe asked Betty when they were back inside.

'Sometimes they go to the hotel across the road and sometimes they bring sandwiches. But they certainly don't sit with us when they bring sandwiches,' she said, laughing. 'They have a little sitting-room of their own.'

Chloe, who spent most of that afternoon rolling bandages, imagined how pleasant it would be to sit under the tree eating lunch with Dr Raven. But obviously that wasn't ever likely to happen.

After work, she and Betty cycled home together, and Chloe felt well satisfied with her first day in her new job.

'Don't you think you'll miss the hospital?' asked Betty. 'It's so much quieter here.'

Chloe and Betty had trained and worked together for several years at a large hospital in London, but then Betty had left to move to the little town of Alderton to live with her aunt, who was of a nervous disposition and had asked Betty to keep her company.

Chloe had remained at the hospital but, reading Betty's frequent letters, had begun to feel envious of her friend's quiet life in the small town practice, and when Betty had told her that Dr Blaine wanted another nurse, she'd jumped at the chance to apply for the position.

'No. I won't miss London or the hospital at all,' she said.

They were cycling past neat little houses with bright, flower-filled gardens.

'You can breathe here. London's traffic gets worse every year.'

'Yes, Alderton's a lovely place to live. But Dr Blaine can be very strict,' warned Betty.

'He certainly seems to have a very large practice. Is he the only doctor in the town?'

'There's Dr Mortimer. He has a practice on the other side of Alderton but he works alone. Dr Blaine likes to be in charge of a large staff. He's ambitious. He's on the town council and I think he hopes to be mayor one day.'

'You said he's a widower?'

'He is. But he has a daughter, Susannah. She's the apple of his eye, as they say. In other words, she's a spoiled madam'

But by this time they'd arrive back at Aunt Ellen's house so there was no more talk of Dr Blaine or Susannah because the older lady was eager for Chloe's news.

'Girls! There you are! It's so lovely to

see you. I've been longing for you to come home. I want to hear all about Chloe's first day.'

Aunt Ellen was small and thin with faded golden hair and faded blue eyes. She had a sweet smile and, usually, an anxious air.

But today she had an excited look. She had some news of her own.

'Have you heard?' she asked.

'Heard what?' asked Betty.

'The Duke and Duchess of York have had a baby girl. Isn't that lovely? She will be called Princess Elizabeth. It's in the newspaper, look!' She seemed as pleased as if the baby had arrived in her own family.

The girls smiled at her excitement.

'Let's just put our hats and coats away and wash our hands and we'll join you for tea,' said Betty.

'Don't be long. I'll ring for it,' said her aunt.

It was rather late for tea but Betty always had a cup with her aunt when she returned from the surgery. Aunt

Ellen spent a lot of each day alone and looked forward to her niece's return with her chat of the outside world. Now she had the pleasure of the company of two girls.

The tea was waiting for them when they returned to the drawing-room.

'And what did you think of Dr Blaine?' Aunt Ellen asked Chloe. 'I believe he's rather a stickler for rules, and that he can be a bit pompous at times, but he's a very good doctor. I always see him myself, not those young men he employs.'

' 'Those young men', as you call them, are very-well-qualified doctors,' Betty reprimanded her aunt.

'I daresay.'

Chloe gazed into her teacup. One of those young men was Dr Raven and she wanted to question Betty about him, but it was very difficult. Her friend would want to know why she was interested and would tease her.

Suddenly she realised Aunt Ellen was asking her a question.

'I'm sorry, I was daydreaming,' she apologised.

'I wondered whether you would find the work at the surgery harder or easier than at the hospital.'

'Well, I don't like to say that I will find it easier, but it will certainly be more enjoyable. At the hospital we were always so busy that we didn't have time to get to know our patients properly.'

They chatted easily for an hour or so then Betty and Chloe rose to go upstairs to change for dinner.

'There's a concert on the wireless at nine o'clock,' Aunt Ellen called after them. 'Shall we listen to it? Do you like music, Chloe?'

'Very much.'

'Actually,' put in Betty, 'I want to take Chloe for a walk around the town after dinner so that she can see where everything is. We'll be back before nine though.'

For the rest of that week, Chloe spent most of her time working in the treatment room while Betty was busy updating patients' notes and records.

Chloe was quite happy to hide away and work in seclusion. Apart from the fact that there was a lot to familiarise herself with in the treatment room, she was nervous of meeting Dr Raven again. The look he had given her with those deep green eyes, and her own reaction to him, had unnerved her.

But she couldn't avoid him forever and one morning, after she'd just finished bandaging the arm of a young gardener who'd hurt himself on a thorny rosebush, Betty came bustling in waving a brown folder.

'Chloe. Could you do me a big favour and take these notes to Dr

Raven? I'd forgotten that he asked me to take them down without fail this morning — and I've just had a call to go to help Dr Blaine in his surgery straight away.'

She thrust the notes at Chloe and rushed off.

Chloe walked slowly down the corridor to Dr Raven's room and knocked hesitantly on the door, expecting to be called inside, but he opened the door himself.

Over his shoulder, Chloe could see that he had a patient — an elderly man — sitting at the side of his desk.

'Oh. It's you!' Adam Raven was obviously disconcerted to see her. 'I'm sorry, Nurse Perle, I'd expected Nurse Wilson. Thank you very much.'

Chloe stepped back and he closed the door.

But his handsome face and his deep green eyes remained in her mind for the rest of that day.

On Saturday afternoon, Chloe declared her intention of spending some time on her own in the town.

'I have to learn to find my own way around,' she said to Betty, 'and I want to join the library and I know you're not interested in reading.'

'I read magazines,' retorted her friend, 'but books take so long. I lose interest. But I want to see Mildred Allen about the tennis club fixtures anyway. So you go to town and I'll see you this evening.'

At the library, Chloe gave her details at the reception desk, received her membership card, and then spent some time browsing the shelves.

The library itself was an ugly Victorian building but it was cool and quiet inside.

After much deliberation, she chose a

couple of detective stories for herself and then went in search of the cookery section. Although Aunt Ellen's maid, Nancy, did most of the cooking, Betty liked to prepare tasty suppers or elaborate cakes when the inclination took her.

Leaving the cookery section after selecting a book about baking, she was so busy flicking through it and looking at the mouth-watering illustrations that she walked headlong into a young man coming from the opposite direction.

'Dr Raven!' She stood quite still, a rich flush diffusing her cheeks.

'Nurse Perle! Fancy seeing you here. You're finding your way around Alderton then?'

She smiled nervously. 'I've found the library anyway. That was my first priority.'

'I take it you're a keen reader?' he said, smiling.

'I am. And you?'

'I read anything and everything. Today it's crime, I'm afraid. I need to relax and a good detective story is a great help.'

'My idea too!'

Chloe held out her two books for his inspection.

They smiled at each other.

'Perhaps we could — I mean, if you're not meeting anyone, perhaps we could have a cup of tea together?' Adam Raven said, looking at her hopefully.

Chloe was glad she'd put on her new blue and white checked dress and the white, close-fitting hat with its delphinium-blue ribbon. She felt she was looking her best.

'That would be lovely,' she said.

She left the choice of teashop to him and he took her to his favourite, a Viennese patisserie.

'What a wonderful selection,' she cried, eyeing the plates and trays of iced and creamy cakes and tarts behind the glass-fronted counter. 'I've never seen a cafè like this before.'

'Quite exotic for Alderton,' he agreed, 'but very popular. So much so that it's sometimes hard to get a table.'

He rested a hand lightly on her back and escorted her towards the rear of the room.

'There are tables overlooking the street but I should hate Dr Blaine to come past and see us together.'

Startled, she stared at him. Was he ashamed of being seen with her? She began to feel uncomfortable.

He noticed her expression and hastened to explain.

'Haven't you been told about Dr Blaine's rules on fraternisation?'

'Fraternisation?'

'Yes. Between members of staff. He believes that if members of the opposite sex who work together get too friendly, then professionalism will suffer.'

'Are you serious?' She stared at him.

At the hospital she had had many friends of both sexes among the staff.

'He's a wonderful doctor, but old-fashioned in many ways,' said Adam. 'I don't challenge his rules, I just find a way to live with them.'

He looked up with a smile for the waitress who was approaching their table.

'What can I get you, sir?'

Adam ordered tea and cakes and they were soon gazing at a delectable selection on a glass cake stand: meringues oozing fresh cream; tartlets piled high with strawberries; sponge cakes glistening with fondant icing; and rich chocolate slices.

Chloe laughed. 'The Viennese certainly have extravagant ideas about cakes!'

'Sometimes I come here and just have a cup of coffee,' he said. 'But today we must celebrate your new position and our lucky meeting.'

Later, they said goodbye outside the teashop. Adam held her hand for a moment in a brief handshake, then turned and was lost amongst the crowd of shoppers.

Chloe was thoughtful as she made her way to a small department store that Betty had pointed out to her the other evening. What was she to make of her meeting with Adam Raven? He had asked her to have coffee with him, yet had pointed out Dr Blaine's rules about friendship between members of staff. Was he warning her not to make too much of their little rendezvous?

Should she mention it to Betty?

She decided to wait and think about it.

The department store was well stocked and she made her way to the materials department. She'd decided to make herself a warmer dress ready for the autumn, and with the help of the saleswoman, she chose a soft, woollen material with narrow green stripes on a pale grey background. She was a good but not spectacular seamstress, so she selected a paper pattern in a simple style. The saleswoman suggested a white pique collar to set it off and, pleased with her purchases, Chloe set off on the fifteen-minute walk home.

When she arrived back, Betty was

already there and was studying her list of tennis club fixtures.

'Mildred and I have spent all afternoon on this,' she said. 'I hope it will be all right.' She looked up at Chloe. 'You'd like to join the tennis club, I expect?'

'Well, perhaps. But I'm not terribly good.'

'I'm sure you're as good as the rest of us,' said Betty kindly. 'I'll take you along on Tuesday evening if you like. Did you find all you wanted in Alderton?'

Chloe produced her dress pattern and the material she'd chosen and Betty and Aunt Ellen — who had by now joined them in the sitting-room — both approved very much of her choice.

'And I know you don't usually like books, but I thought you might like one that's filled with pictures of cakes?' Chloe said to her friend, laughing as she handed her the library book of recipes.

'Oh, how wonderful!' cried Aunt Ellen. 'Nancy is a marvellous plain cook but she can't beat Betty at baking!'

'I shall insist on trying out all of these recipes on the two of you,' Betty told them. 'So it will be your own faults if you get fat!'

Then they went upstairs to change for dinner.

As she brushed her hair, Chloe studied her reflection in the mirror and wondered whether Adam Raven had liked what he'd seen across the tea table that afternoon.

Should she tell Betty about the visit to the patisserie?

She went downstairs deciding that it would keep for another time.

On Monday morning, when Chloe went to collect the list of that morning's patients from Miss Jenkins, she noticed a tall, slim girl in a very chic low-waisted dress, straightening the piles of magazines and papers in the waiting-room.

As Chloe entered, the girl was just turning her attention to a vase of rather limp roses and she smiled at Chloe.

'Do you think fresh water would help or shall I get some new flowers?' she asked.

Chloe looked at her blankly.

'Oh, I'm sorry,' the other girl said and held out a hand. 'I'm Susannah Blaine. You must be the new nurse?'

A shaft of early sunshine through the side window lit up Susannah's red-gold hair and the light dusting of freckles on her nose. She was very pretty.

'Chloe Perle,' Chloe introduced herself. 'You're not here instead of Miss Jenkins, are you?'

'Good gracious, no.' Susannah laughed. 'I'm afraid I'm amusing myself pretending to be a working girl.'

At the look on Chloe's face, she realised that perhaps having to earn a living was no joke.

'I'm sorry, I'm always saying the wrong thing. It's my father's idea. I want to have a career — I don't really know what at, to be honest — but Father says that looking after his household is work enough for me. He's arranged for me to spend a week at the surgery doing different jobs so that I can see what it's like to be out all day.'

'How do you feel about that?' asked Chloe.

'Well, medical work definitely isn't what I had in mind! I think perhaps that I should like to train as a teacher. I'm good with children. I'm sure I could do it.'

Looking at the other girl's colourful

elegance, Chloe found it hard to imagine her doing anything other than wafting around looking pretty.

Susannah sighed. 'I expect Father's right. I'd probably hate having to go out to work once the novelty had worn off. I do like my freedom.'

Before Chloe could reply, Miss Jenkins came into the room and handed her the list of patients. She glanced at the list, then said goodbye to Susannah and returned to the treatment room.

On Mondays and Tuesdays, Dr Raven was out a great deal on house calls so his own and Chloe's paths had no opportunity to cross.

But if he'd really wanted to see her he could have created an opportunity, she thought sadly. Perhaps she was making too much out of a pleasant chat in a teashop. He'd probably just been being kind.

That Tuesday evening, she set off with Betty for the tennis club, determined to make some new friends. There were several courts so she looked forward to getting a game.

She and Betty knocked a ball around for a while, and Chloe felt she was playing reasonably well. Then two other girls joined them in a game of doubles.

Afterwards, they returned to the club-house for a much needed cool drink and were soon joined by a young man.

'Tom Clive,' Betty said, introducing him. 'My brother's oldest friend. Tom, this is Chloe.'

Tom was plump and smiling.

'Let's try a mixed doubles,' he said to Betty, 'you and me against Chloe and . . . who can we get? Oh, of course!' He waved. 'Adam! Over here!'

Chloe looked in the direction in which Tom was waving and saw a tall, familiar figure pushing his way through the crowd to join the group.

'We need another man to partner Chloe,' said Tom.

'Hello again,' said Adam.

'So you two know each other?'

'Chloe,' Adam smiled at her as if seeking permission to use her Christian name, 'has recently joined the surgery. She's our new nurse.'

'So, as a trainee solicitor and a non-medical man, I'm the odd one out. Never mind. Come on, let's bag a court.'

Tom led the way outside and he and Betty took their places at the far side of the net.

'I hope I won't let you down,' said Chloe to Adam, wondering whether he was a very good player.

'I'm sure we'll make a fine pair,' he said, smiling.

The game was fast and fun, and although Betty and Tom won, Chloe was happy with the way she'd played.

Adam praised her when they'd finished, draping her sweater round her shoulders and putting his arm casually around her waist as they walked to the club-house.

Her cup of happiness was full to the brim and overflowing.

'What about making a foursome one evening and going to the Pelican?' Tom suggested. 'The food is good there and they have a jazz band. Do you like jazz?'

The two girls looked at each other.

'I don't think I know what it is,' Betty confessed.

'It's the latest popular music from America,' Adam explained. 'You've never heard music like it. It's — oh, I can't describe it! You'll have to come and hear it.'

'Sounds fun,' said Chloe, her eyes shining.

'We'll have to arrange an evening sometime soon!' Tom was excited at the prospect. 'Oh! Do you really have to go?' he added in dismay as he saw that the girls were putting on their coats and hats.

'We have to be up bright and early,' Betty reminded him.

'I have to go now, too. I'll walk you back,' said Adam.

\* \* \*

Aunt Ellen was in bed when they reached home, so Betty opened the door with her latchkey and the two girls crept towards the kitchen.

'Warm milk?' Betty took a small saucepan from the cupboard.

Once it was heated through she poured the milk into two cups and they carried them upstairs.

'Come in here while we drink it.' She opened the door to her bedroom and perched on the bed while Chloe sat in the armchair.

'It was a good evening, wasn't it?' Chloe said, smiling.

'You got on very well with Adam,' commented her friend.

Chloe was thoughtfully silent for a while.

'He's very attractive,' she said at last. 'Actually — ' She paused. 'I didn't mention it before, but I had coffee with him in town that day I went to the library.'

'You sly thing!' Betty was amused. 'Why didn't you tell me?'

'I . . . don't know.'

She felt the warmth beginning to rise in her cheeks and bent her head to take a sip from her mug of milk.

'Oh, dear! You haven't fallen for him, have you?' asked Betty.

'Would it matter if I had?'

'I'm afraid it would.' Her friend looked at her with a serious expression on her face. 'You see, quite apart from the fact that — even under normal circumstances — it wouldn't do either of you any good career-wise if Dr Blaine found out that you were meeting socially, the fact that Susannah Blaine has her eye on Adam definitely makes it a bad idea! I know that the two of them sometimes go out together and that her father encourages their friendship. It wouldn't do for you to tread on Susannah's toes, Chloe. It really wouldn't.'

'But you and I have arranged to go as a foursome to a jazz club with Adam and Tom!' said Chloe, puzzled. 'You didn't make any objection to that!'

'That's different. That's just chums going on an outing,' Betty explained. 'And even though Dr Blaine wouldn't approve even of that, he's hardly likely to find out about it. What I'm telling you is not to go falling for Adam or getting involved with him romantically in any way. Nothing can ever come of it while the two of you are working at the surgery, and even if you weren't, then I suspect that Adam is attracted to Susannah because of who she is, rather than for her own sake. After all, think how advantageous it would be for him to be married to his boss's daughter! Keep clear, Chloe. He'll only break your heart.'

# A Disappointment For Chloe

Next day there was a tap at the treatment room door and Chloe looked up just as Susannah Blaine called out, 'Hello-o!' and came right in, closing the door behind her.

She was wearing a white dress and looked rather like an angel.

'Sorry. You've got me for a few days.'

Chloe looked puzzled and Susannah hurried to explain.

'You remember I said I was spending time helping at the surgery to see if I'd like to go out to work? Well, I'm with you today.'

She pointed down at her dress, her expression wry. 'Nearest thing I could find to a uniform.'

Chloe gave her a tight little smile. 'I'll get Betty,' she said. 'She'll tell you what to do.'

Betty was busy in the stockroom

arranging bottles of liquid paraffin, digitalis, and willow, some of the ingredients from which the doctors would make the draughts they prescribed.

'We've got help this week,' Chloe told her unemotionally. 'Susannah Blaine's here to give us a hand.'

Betty looked at her. 'I knew she was coming. Don't look so mad. It's not the end of the world. We'll survive.'

'I can't be friendly with her as if I didn't mind about . . . about Adam,' Chloe whispered fiercely. 'And she's such a spoiled brat!'

'Don't jeopardise your job,' Betty warned. 'Dr Blaine idolises Susannah. For goodness' sake don't upset her.'

She carefully replaced the lid on a box of bandages and stretched up to put it on the top shelf.

'Dr Ramsden wants a nurse to go with him on house calls both this morning and tomorrow morning. That will get you away from the surgery. Now — smile!'

They returned to the treatment room and Chloe collected her hat and coat before thankfully making her way down the corridor to Dr Ramsden's room.

There followed two mornings away from her usual routine and she was amazed at how many patients they visited. Dr Ramsden didn't rush, but his quiet efficiency meant that they were in and out of each house in good time.

She helped him in various ways — with bandaging and injections, holding babies, and in the last house they visited, comforting a confused old woman.

Dr Ramsden nodded in approval as they left that house.

'You're a good nurse,' he said. 'You've got the right attitude, sensible but sympathetic.'

She felt that, coming from him, that was praise indeed.

On her first lunch-time back at the practice the weather was warm and sunny and the three girls took their lunch into the garden.

Susannah turned to Chloe while Betty was away making the tea.

'You didn't hear about my party, did you? I was telling Betty all about it yesterday morning.'

'Party?'

'Mm. My twentieth. It was last Saturday.'

Obviously overjoyed to have found a fresh audience, she chattered on excitedly about the food and the presents, but when she came to talking about the guests, Chloe felt she didn't want to hear any more. She had a horrible feeling she knew what was coming next.

'Dr Raven and Dr Ramsden came — or Adam and Gordon, I should say!' Susannah giggled. 'It was very naughty of me but I danced mostly with Adam. He's a wonderful dancer.'

She stared dreamily up into the branches of the tree above her.

'Of course, he's not my boyfriend. Only a friend.'

She gave Chloe a sly sideways look,

36

as though trying to decide whether to confide in her.

But before she could say any more, Betty arrived back with the tea tray, along with Miss Garland and Miss Jenkins.

'Do you remember when we were in that Christmas revue while we were still at the hospital?' Betty asked as they cycled home one evening.

'Rather!' Chloe laughed at the memory. 'We couldn't remove all the stage make-up before we went to the party afterwards!'

'Well, I was thinking,' Betty went on, 'would you like to come along to my drama group?'

'Drama group? Oh, I don't know. Performing in a few short sketches was one thing, but acting in a play . . . '

'Oh, but we don't perform anything highbrow — just light comedies and sometimes thrillers. It's great fun. Why don't you come along just to watch? If you wanted to help out, then you could make the tea,' said Betty. 'Who knows, you might even decide to try for a little part.'

Two evenings later, Chloe found herself in the local church hall in the centre of a group of excited amateur thespians. The new play was being cast and everyone was anxious for a part — everyone except Chloe, who sat quietly at the back of the hall.

The play, a frivolous comedy, was being produced by Tom Clive, Betty's brother's friend. He was pleased to see Chloe again, but she hastened to warn him that she was there as a tea-maker, not an actress.

He gave her a smile and a 'we'll see' sort of look.

During the tea-break, Chloe carried round plates of biscuits and when she got to a small group consisting of Tom, Betty and a few others, an argument was in progress.

' . . . only a small part, but quite important,' Tom was saying, 'and she must be a blonde.'

'She could wear a wig,' Betty pointed out. 'We have a few brunettes left without parts.'

Tom looked around the room. 'Too old,' he objected. 'And I don't like wigs, they're not life-like.' His glance fell on Chloe as she proffered the plate of biscuits.

'Nurse Perle! A natural blonde, as I live and breathe!'

Chloe looked startled.

'Only twelve lines,' Tom wheedled. 'You can remember twelve lines.'

Betty joined in with the persuading. 'Please, Chloe. You'd be perfect.'

At last Chloe gave in and went home clutching her copy of the play and the hope that she wouldn't make a fool of herself.

Seeing the girls at the drama group had reminded Tom that he'd suggested a visit to the jazz club and so he'd contacted Adam.

When the girls arrived at the church hall for the next rehearsal, Tom approached them straight away and asked if they were free that Friday evening.

'We'll call for you at eight,' he said.

Betty looked at Chloe and was amused to see that her friend was blushing.

'That will be wonderful, Tom. We'll look forward to it.'

Tom moved away and called everyone to attention, and so Chloe — who had suddenly become the colour of a beetroot — was spared the embarrassment of being teased by Betty.

It was Chloe's first rehearsal. She'd learned her twelve lines and was feeling quite confident about them. She felt less confident about what she had to do on the stage, however, because the stage directions in her script called for a kiss. She hoped that was just a suggestion. She'd feel dreadful if she had to kiss a stranger, and in front of all these people, too.

She looked nervously around at the crowd of actors.

'Henry.' Tom was calling a young man over. 'This is Chloe. You're playing opposite her.'

Henry was a thin, almost bald, and very earnest young man who was looking as nervous as she was. They smiled at each other uncertainly.

'Go and stand together in front of the park bench,' Tom directed, pointing at the stage.

Chloe climbed the steps first. Please don't let me have to kiss him, she prayed silently.

Somehow they got through their lines to Tom's satisfaction and there was no mention of a kiss.

She breathed again.

'That wasn't too bad, was it?' Betty asked when they were at home and drinking a bedtime cup of cocoa. 'Tom was really pleased with you.'

Chloe said nothing. She took her cup to the sink and washed it.

'Can we talk tomorrow, Betty?' she asked. 'I'm very tired.'

'Of course. And we must decide what to wear on Saturday. Do you think . . . '

But Chloe had already left the room.

Chloe's first impression of the Pelican Club was that it was dreadfully smoky. There was a blue haze across the room and she tried hard not to cough as they made their way to a table.

Adam held a chair for her to sit down. 'I hope we can see from here,' he said.

'It was the best table they had at short notice,' Tom apologised.

Chloe looked around. The room was packed with young people all chatting excitedly. They were all drinking and most were smoking. She stared in surprise as Betty drew a cigarette case from her bag. She had never seen her friend smoke before.

The men each accepted a cigarette when Betty handed round the case but Chloe drew back with a shake of her head.

'You don't?' asked Adam. 'It steadies the nerves, but I'm sure your nerves are quite steady already.'

How wrong you are, she thought. Sitting next to Adam as if it was the most natural thing in the world and trying to chat casually, was *very* trying on the nerves.

She was glad when a waitress came to take their drinks order.

'Shall we try the new American drinks?' Tom suggested. 'They're called cocktails.'

Betty giggled. 'What a funny name.'

'What's in them?' asked Chloe.

Tom looked enquiringly at the waitress.

'Gin and vermouth,' she said.

'We'll try them,' said Adam, deciding for them all. 'We're listening to music from America so we might as well have drinks from America.'

'I believe the jazz dancers are genuine Americans, too,' said Tom, and he began to say something else but his words were drowned out by the sharp wail of a trombone.

Betty and Chloe looked at each other in surprise as the tune was taken up and elaborated upon by other members of the band. The girls had never heard anything like it.

Suddenly four men in bright clothes burst into the space in the centre of the room and began to fling themselves in all directions in time to the music.

Adam was tapping his fingers on the table in time to the beat.

He gave Chloe a wide smile but there was too much noise to say anything.

The trombonist was standing up now and the notes he was playing cascaded up and down the scales.

The dance became wilder, the music louder. Suddenly there was a crescendo of sound, enthusiastic applause, and the dancers collapsed in splits on to the dance floor.

Chloe and Betty clapped as loudly and wildly as everyone else.

'Wasn't that good?' enthused Betty. 'Oh, I hope they do some more.'

'They will later,' Adam promised. 'Now it's our turn.'

He stood up, turned to Chloe and held out a hand.

'I can't do anything like that!' she told him, giggling.

'I don't think anyone would expect you to,' he said solemnly. 'We'll be old-fashioned and just do the foxtrot.'

To Chloe, the evening was a blur of sound and activity. She danced with Adam, then Tom, then again with Adam. There was a break for supper, another performance from the professional dancers, and then she was on the dance floor again with Adam for the last waltz.

'I have enjoyed this evening,' she murmured into his neck as he held her close. 'I've never been to anything like this before but it's been such fun.'

Adam held her away from him and studied her face. 'Your eyes are shining and so is your nose.' He laughed. 'You certainly look as if you've enjoyed yourself.'

'I shall be very sleepy in the morning. I wonder if Betty's Aunt Ellen will mind if we lie in for a while?'

'I'm sure she won't. She was young herself once, though I don't suppose she ever worked for a living.'

They continued to circle the room.

'I'd hoped you might need to change your library book tomorrow,' Adam said after a while. 'But of course, if you need to stay in bed . . . '

'You've just reminded me.' Chloe gave him a cheeky smile. 'I do have a book to return.'

'So if I happened to be returning my book at about half-past ten, you might be there at the library, too?'

'I might,' she agreed.

'And afterwards, if you have nothing else to do, perhaps we could have coffee and a cake?'

The dance came to an end. They joined in with the applause, then made their way back to their table.

★　★　★

'See you for rehearsal on Tuesday,' Tom reminded the girls as the four young people parted at Aunt Ellen's gate.

'Rehearsal?' queried Adam.

'I have a tiny part in a play,' Chloe told him. 'Tom's producing it.'

Adam studied her but said nothing.

The girls made their way into the house, excited and trying to subdue their giggles.

'What a fabulous evening!' said Chloe. 'And what about those cocktails?'

'I didn't like them very much,' Betty admitted, 'but that didn't matter. We were being very fashionable.'

They removed their shoes at the bottom of the stairs to creep up quietly.

'Adam's a good dancer, isn't he?' said Betty. 'Susannah said he was.'

'Did you have to mention Susannah and ruin the evening?' asked Chloe, only half joking.

Betty put her hands on her friend's shoulders.

'I don't want you to forget what I

said and get hurt,' she said quietly. 'Susannah has ideas about Adam Raven. And what Susannah wants, Susannah usually gets.'

At the rehearsal on Tuesday, Henry — the young man who'd played opposite Chloe the week before — was missing.

When Tom arrived, he looked cross.

'He's pulled out,' he said. 'At this late stage! Had to go to London for three weeks, he said. I don't believe him. Found something better to do, I expect.'

He stood looking around the group. 'You'll have to step into the part, Malcolm,' he said to a tall, thin young man who was busy at the back of the stage with some scenery.

'Oh, no, I won't,' Malcolm refused fiercely. 'I'm not an actor. You'll just have to do it yourself, Tom.'

Chloe looked at Tom who smiled back.

'Don't worry, Chloe, we'll sort

something out. I'll read the part just for this evening.'

The rehearsal started and because her own character didn't come on until Act Two, Chloe settled down to watch.

She thought that everyone was actually rather good. But her thoughts kept drifting away from the play and slipping back to the previous Saturday morning. Adam had already been at the library when she'd arrived.

They'd chosen their books quickly and were soon out in the sunshine, walking automatically to the Viennese patisserie.

'Tell me about your play,' Adam had said after they'd ordered their coffee and cakes. 'Are you a good character or a bad character?'

'It's a very small part,' she'd admitted. 'I just have to meet my boyfriend at a park bench and have a bit of an argument. I have so few lines, I don't think it matters whether I'm good or bad.'

'Have you done a lot of acting?'

'No. Almost none! It was Betty who persuaded me to do it. I went along just to meet people and to make the tea and I was coaxed into taking the part. Have you done any acting, Adam?'

'Only at school. And I'm too busy now. But I'll come and see the play.'

'Mm. You'll be able to see me forgetting all of my twelve lines!'

'You won't forget any of your lines, you'll be very good. They'll probably give you the lead in the next production.'

She'd pretended to hide behind her coffee cup but had looked at him surreptitiously over the rim.

At the surgery, he was very correct, only speaking to her when necessary and then with a strictly professional air. No-one would have guessed that they were friends away from work.

But it *was* only friendship, or at least, so it seemed on his part. But Chloe had realised that she was falling deeper and deeper in love with him.

She'd been aching to ask him

whether he took Susannah Blaine out very often. But how could she mention the other girl? He'd know she'd been discussing him. He'd wonder why. And if he asked, would she say, because I love you and the thought of you with Susannah is more than I can bear?

'Would you like some more coffee?' she'd asked him, busying herself with the coffee pot to cover her confusion.

Coffee! Chloe had been so deep in her memories of the previous Saturday that she'd forgotten that she was the official tea-maker to the drama group! She crept from her seat and into the little kitchen to fill the kettle and put out a row of cups and saucers.

It was a few days later and afternoon surgery had just finished. Betty was putting the used linen in a bag for the laundry and Chloe was filing patients' records, when there was a knock at the door of the treatment room.

When it opened, both girls were surprised to see that it was Adam standing there.

'Dr Raven. Can we help you?'

'I wanted to speak to you both.' He looked slightly embarrassed. 'Do the two of you possess such garments as ballgowns?'

Chloe gave him a funny look.

'Ballgowns? You mean, as in Cinderella?'

'I mean, do you both have evening dresses suitable for a rather grand dance?'

Chloe looked at Betty. 'Well — no. I

don't really go anywhere to wear that sort of thing.'

Betty shook her head. 'Neither do I.'

'Well, could you both get suitable dance dresses by Friday week?'

'What's this all about?'

'You're both going to a ball! With Dr Blaine!'

Chloe was speechless, then she gave a little laugh.

'Very funny. Well, you can tell Dr Blaine that we're very sorry, but we're not allowed to fraternise with him!'

Adam came right into the room, closing the door behind him.

'Let me explain. Dr Blaine has bought tickets to take a large party to the Charity Ball at the Town Hall. Dr Ramsden and I have been given two each and we intend to tell Dr Blaine that we are asking you both to come as our partners — as a reward for your hard work for us.'

'But he won't agree — will he?'

'We intend to put it to him in such a way that he can't refuse without sounding really mean.'

'Don't yourself and Dr Ramsden have anyone else that you'd rather take?' asked Betty.

'Dr Ramsden and I are very happy with the idea of escorting our lovely young nurses to a dance,' said Adam firmly.

On Saturday morning, an excited pair of girls set off for the shops in search of two dresses that were glamorous enough to amaze the guests at the Town Hall.

'My aunt has a good dressmaker,' said Betty, as they hurried along. 'We could get some material and have them made. There's time.'

'Let's try on some ready-made dresses first,' said Chloe. 'Then we'll know what suits us.'

'I wonder what Dr Blaine said when Adam told him that he'd invited us? Oh, to have been a fly on the wall.' Chloe giggled.

'Didn't Adam tell you what he said?'

'No. He just said that Dr Blaine had agreed. So I took it that he wasn't too pleased. Anyway, I intend to enjoy myself in spite of him.'

They reached the doors of Alderton's main department store and hurried inside. The model gown salon was on the second floor.

'The sales assistants look very grand,' whispered Betty. 'Perhaps the dresses will be too expensive for us.'

'Shh,' said Chloe as a tall, stiff-looking woman dressed in black approached. Chloe explained what they wanted.

They were waved to a couch while the saleswoman and a young assistant disappeared for a few minutes, then came back, each carrying an armful of clothes.

The girls sat up, eyes shining.

The saleswoman eyed their short dresses.

'I imagine you don't want *very* short evening dresses.'

'Oh no,' Chloe hastened to assure her. 'Fashionable, but not short.'

'Because we do have short skirts with long floating panels.'

A red dress was held up.

They looked at each other.

'Dr Blaine wouldn't like that,' whispered Betty.

'We mustn't be too unconventional,' said Chloe. 'Could we see that grey one, please?'

The grey dress was held up but the girls shook their heads. Then the junior displayed an ice blue satin.

Chloe stood up to look more closely at it.

'Oh, I like that. May I try it on?' she asked and was led away to a curtained area.

She was back in ten minutes, twirling in front of Betty to display the dress's very low draped back that ended in a heavy bow. It was sleeveless and had a wide neck.

Betty clapped her hands. 'You must have it. It's absolutely you.'

Chloe admired herself in the long looking-glass.

'Er . . . how much . . . ' she asked nervously.

The saleswoman murmured a figure and Chloe tried not to blink. She made some rapid calculations. She could just afford it, and it had to be an investment. Even Dr Blaine would be impressed.

While Chloe was changing and the gown was being carefully wrapped in layers of tissue paper, Betty inspected the other dresses but she shook her head at Chloe when she reappeared.

'Nothing for me, I'm afraid. Let's try Marcelle Modes, they have some quite nice things in their windows.'

At Marcelle Modes they were greeted by a tiny lady who was dressed all in red and who had startlingly black hair which looked as if it had been painted on to her head. She made Chloe think of a wooden doll.

Betty explained what she wanted and found herself being appraised by black, beady eyes.

'You are dark. Red would suit you. But it's rather obvious. What about this instead?'

She turned to a rack of clothes against the wall and selected a dress, sweeping it across the carpet so that

Betty could appreciate the detail.

It was black with tiny sleeves, embroidered and beaded in white, with a deep band of the same decoration around the hips.

'But it's so . . . elegant,' gasped Betty. 'Do you think I could really wear something like that?'

The small woman whisked back the curtain from a changing cubicle in the corner of the room.

'Try it on,' she invited. 'I think you will be surprised.'

Betty did as she suggested and came out wearing the dress, looking shy and embarrassed, which was surprising for her, thought Chloe.

'Stand up straight,' the woman instructed. 'Think yourself elegant'.

'There!' She pointed at Betty's reflection in the long glass. 'With the right shoes and a little rouge and lipstick . . . '

'What do you think?' Betty asked Chloe.

'You look very different. Not like

yourself at all,' her friend admitted. 'But you could certainly carry it off.'

Betty appraised her reflection again.

'I'll have it,' she decided. 'I'll be elegant if it kills me.'

As they walked home, a thought struck Chloe.

'If they're such friends and she's so keen on him, why isn't Adam escorting Susannah Blaine to the dance?'

'I forgot to tell you,' said Betty. 'She's going to Scotland for a month. Miss Jenkins told me.'

Chloe didn't know whether to be relieved at this news — because it meant that she would have Adam to herself at the dance — or upset, because she suspected that if Susannah had been at home Adam would never even have considered inviting Chloe.

They'd started on the final week of rehearsals for the play. When Betty and Chloe walked into the church hall that evening, Tom was talking to someone near the stage. The two men turned to smile as the girls came in and Chloe was appalled to see that Tom's companion was Adam. How could she remember her lines if he was watching?

Tom called her over.

'Chloe, I'm not happy about both directing the play and acting the part. So I've found another actor to play opposite you.'

Chloe looked at Adam in amazement.

'You're going to play the part? But you said you can't act.'

'Tom has persuaded me I can manage a small part like this. And I've only got ten lines to your twelve.'

He gave her an encouraging smile.

'Come on, let's find a corner where we can practice.'

Adam already knew his part and Chloe found him very easy to respond to.

For the first time, she began to wish she had a longer scene!

# Chloe Dances On Air

There were to be two public perfor-
mances of the play and, waiting in the
wings for her cue on the first night,
Chloe realised that the next five
minutes spent playing one short scene
with Adam would be one of the
highlights of her week.

She could see him in the wings
opposite. Then their cue came, and they
were on stage.

Losing all nervousness, Chloe
remembered all her moves; flouncing
and stamping and feeling that she
really was the very cross fiancée.

Adam, in turn, acted impeccably.

At the end of the scene, he swung her
into his arms, gave her a long,
passionate kiss, and strode off.

Chloe looked after him, amazed, her
face scarlet with embarrassment as the
audience shouted and whistled.

He was waiting for her as she came off the stage.

'I'm sorry,' he said. 'I got a bit carried away. And the script did say they kiss at the end.'

Chloe couldn't think of anything to say to him. He didn't look at all sorry; in fact, he looked quite pleased with himself.

'You could have warned me,' she muttered.

The next night she was prepared, and Adam looked startled in his turn at her response to his kiss.

I'll teach him to go out with Susannah Blaine, she thought, as she marched off the stage.

The play was a great success. When it was over, the actors stood in a line, receiving the congratulations of the audience.

Chloe felt wrapped in a warm glow of satisfaction.

'And now we have the ball to look forward to in just a few days' time,' said Betty, as they returned to the dressing-room for their bags.

No-one saw exactly what happened, but as Chloe was descending the steps from the stage, she fell, twisting her ankle beneath her.

Betty, just behind, rushed to help, but Chloe was unable to get up and her face was contorted with pain.

Someone called out for a doctor, and Adam, full of concern, rushed to her side. He gently manipulated her foot and declared it a sprain but not a break.

Chloe was carried out to Tom's car and, with Betty and Adam in attendance, she was taken home.

Once there, Adam carefully strapped up the ankle and assured Aunt Ellen that the patient would be back to normal in a week.

'But you'll need to rest it for a few days,' he warned her. 'No walking on it.'

After he'd gone, Chloe turned a tragic face to Betty. 'Oh, Betty. No walking — so definitely no dancing. I shan't be able to go to the ball.'

Chloe spent the following week lying on the sitting-room couch, resting her strapped ankle while Aunt Ellen waited upon her. The old lady was sorry for her but pleased to have company all day.

Chloe, though, missing the surgery, was desperate to get back to work.

Adam called to see her several times. 'You're doing well,' he said, 'but no returning to work until Monday.'

Monday! But the ball was on Saturday!

Betty said that if Chloe couldn't go then she wouldn't go either. They had quite an argument over it.

Asked for her opinion, Aunt Ellen said she thought Betty *should* go.

'If you don't, then there'll be no one to tell us all about it. And think of those two poor young men without even one partner between them.'

Partner! Would Adam find someone else to take? Chloe allowed herself a little smile at the thought of him escorting Miss Jenkins.

On Saturday night, Betty, feeling guilty that she was the one to be going out, protested again.

'I really don't mind staying home with you.'

'Betty, please! You're making me feel worse. The accident was due to my own carelessness. Why should you suffer?'

Chloe was lying on the sofa and she glanced up at the clock on the mantelpiece.

'They'll be here to collect you in three-quarters of an hour. Go and get ready. And don't forget to take note of everything that happens,' she called after Betty as she left the room.

When Betty presented herself for their inspection, Chloe and Aunt Ellen nodded approvingly.

The glistening black dress fell in a

column to her ankles. Small diamanté clips on the front of her black satin shoes matched the decoration on her clutch bag, and she also wore a diamanté edged comb in her gleaming hair — but no jewellery. The decoration on the dress was enough.

'Dr Blaine won't believe his eyes,' said Chloe. 'You've done it! That's real elegance!'

There was a ring at the doorbell and a few moments later Aunt Ellen's maid showed in the two doctors who were immaculate in evening dress.

Dr Ramsden made polite conversation to Aunt Ellen while Adam bent over Chloe.

'I'm so sorry,' he murmured, 'but we'll make up for it when your ankle is better and we'll go dancing, just the two of us.'

Chloe gave him a brave smile. 'Off you go,' she said. 'You mustn't be late.'

Betty bent to kiss her and as the three revellers left the room, tears began to roll down Chloe's cheeks.

'There is to be a play on the wireless at eight-thirty,' said Aunt Ellen, pretending not to notice. 'I think perhaps we'll listen to that together.'

On Monday morning, Chloe, her ankle firmly bandaged and with a stick to give support, hobbled into work.

Betty had told her very little about the Charity Ball. She'd obviously enjoyed herself, but had not dwelt too long on the delights, probably because she felt awkward that Chloe hadn't been there to share them.

In the treatment room, Chloe did most of the sitting down jobs and she was at the desk studying the list of the morning's patients when Dr Blaine appeared. He seemed in a good mood.

'Pity you missed the Charity Ball,' he said. 'Dr Raven said you were to be his partner. How's the ankle?'

'Getting better, thank you,' said Chloe.

'Yes, pity you missed it,' he repeated, 'but Dr Raven was all right after all. My naughty daughter saw to that.'

'Susannah?' Chloe looked at him in surprise. 'I thought she was in Scotland.'

'So she was. But when she heard about the ball, she had to go to it! So she came home unexpectedly for the weekend. Went back to Scotland this morning.'

He smiled fondly. 'She really is a little minx. I fixed her up with a nice partner, the son of a friend of mine, but he didn't suit the young madam. Once she saw Adam she made a bee-line for him and left the young lad high and dry. We'll have a romance on our hands soon with those two, you'll see.'

He left the room chuckling to himself.

Betty had come in just in time to hear the end of this conversation and she looked at her friend's stricken face.

'You told me Susannah wasn't going,' Chloe scolded her. 'Why didn't you say she was there after all?'

'I didn't want to upset you,' said

Betty miserably. 'I hoped you wouldn't find out.'

'And she danced with Adam all night?'

'Mmm . . . '

'You were right, Betty. I've been a fool about Adam. I know he's not given me any encouragement to feel the way I do, but he must realise that I see him as more than a friend! And then there's the way he kissed me when we were in the play together! That *certainly* didn't feel as if he was acting! But I've learned my lesson. I'll keep my distance from him from now on, I swear.'

Two weeks later, Adam called Chloe into his consulting room. 'Is the ankle quite better now?'

'Oh yes, it's fine. No pain at all. Thank you for asking.'

'Well, I was wondering whether it was healed enough for dancing? I think I owe you an evening out to make up for the one you missed.'

After making up her mind to keep her distance from him, Chloe had hoped he'd forgotten his promise to take her out.

Now she forgot all her resolutions and smiled happily.

'Oh, I'm sure my ankle's strong enough for dancing!'

'And you'll wear your new dress?'

'Well, it is a bit . . . dressy. Where are we . . . ?'

'What about the Belmont? Will that be dressy enough for the dress?'

'The Belmont?' breathed Chloe, her mind a whirl. The Belmont was the grandest hotel in the area.

Adam collected a file from the shelf and tucked it under his arm.

'I have to see Dr Blaine about Mrs Agnew. I'll call for you at seven-thirty on Saturday,' he told her. And with that, he was gone.

Chloe closed his door and made her way back to the treatment room.

'What's happened?' asked Betty. 'You look as if you've found treasure.'

Chloe gazed at her with starry eyes.

'Adam's taking me to The Belmont on Saturday. I'm wearing my new blue dress.' She sat down suddenly. 'It was almost worth getting a sprained ankle to have this as a consolation.'

'Oh, do take that idiotic smile off your face,' Betty said in mock exasperation. 'Any one would think you were going out with the Prince of Wales!'

'I'd rather go out with Adam than the Prince of Wales,' said Chloe, dreamily. 'There'll be just the two of us. We'll dance, and he'll take me for a stroll in the gardens in the moonlight.'

'Just remember you're a well brought up young lady and don't go wandering off into the shrubbery,' warned Betty.

'Adam's not like that,' Chloe protested. 'He'll be a perfect gentleman no matter where we are.' She stood up. 'Now, where are those bottles of medicine Dr Blaine prepared? I must label them and put them on the shelf for collection.'

Betty handed her the bottles and gave her an affectionate smile.

'Don't take any notice of my teasing,' she said. 'But seriously, please be careful. Adam Raven is not for you, Chloe — don't let him break your heart.'

The Chateau Belmont had been built in the nineteenth century by a wealthy businessman for his homesick French wife.

Chloe had passed it many times and been fascinated by the pointed roofs and fairy-tale towers. It was a perfect French chateau in the English country-side.

Set back from the road, it was reached by a winding drive which crossed ornamental bridges over a picturesque narrow river.

Now, in the dusk, the brightly-lit windows threw a golden light over the lawns and gardens. Flower borders were spot-lit, tiny lanterns decorated the trees. The whole scene had an unreal, magical air.

Inside, the dining room was huge, illuminated by sparkling chandeliers.

Chloe and Adam followed the waiter to a table set into one of the oriel windows overlooking the garden.

'Isn't it beautiful?' she whispered to Adam. 'I've never had dinner in such a grand place.'

Another waiter approached and handed them each a tasselled menu.

Chloe knew some French, but this completely bewildered her. *Poulet* meant chicken, *agneau* was lamb — but what on earth did the rest of it mean?

Feeling foolish, she looked helplessly at Adam.

He guessed the problem. 'Would you like me to order for you? Is there anything you don't like?'

'Well, if the cooking is all French then I don't think I want snails or frogs' legs,' she admitted shyly.

'I shouldn't dream or ordering those for you,' he told her, smiling.

He and the waiter had a long discussion, then the wine waiter was called forward.

Goodness, thought Chloe, what a

performance for a meal.

At last the discussions ended and the men departed.

'They take food very seriously here,' said Adam.

Another waiter appeared and poured out aperitifs, then at last they were alone. They smiled at each other and Chloe examined her surroundings.

She was so pleased to discover that her dress was the equal of any other there that evening. Feeling more confident, she sat up straight and sipped her drink.

'Is this grander than the Town Hall?' she asked.

'You're thinking of the Charity Ball? Well, they'd made the Town Hall look very nice for the evening. And, of course, it's full of impressive oil paintings and marble floors and staircases, but I prefer this.'

'Then I'm glad I came here instead,' she said with satisfaction.

Their first course arrived; grilled prawns in a delicate lemon sauce with thin slices of bread and butter.

Chloe ate slowly to relish the taste.

Adam smiled at her obvious enjoyment.

'What would you be eating at home tonight?'

'Betty cooks on Saturday nights if we don't go out. She loves cooking and it's always something adventurous.'

'Can you cook?'

'I can, but I don't particularly enjoy it,' she admitted, hoping he wouldn't think her a useless girl. 'Anyway, Betty is so good, I shouldn't like the comparison.'

'I can cook,' he said, surprisingly, 'and I enjoy it.'

'Really? That's unusual for a man.'

'I had a French grandmother. She taught me.'

'That will be useful when you're married,' said Chloe, then wished she hadn't and hastily changed the subject. 'How long have you been at the surgery?'

They talked shop until the next course arrived.

The lamb was exquisite and melted in the mouth. There were minute potatoes and tiny peas. A velvety sauce, redolent of mint, accompanied the dish.

'I wonder whether they ate food like this when it was a private house?' Chloe mused. 'It's delicious.'

'Oh, I should think they ate very well indeed. He was a very wealthy man and she was a French lady; she'd appreciate good food.'

'Do you know what happened to them?'

'It was very sad. She was unhappy away from her homeland, even in her beautiful chateau. She returned to France and was killed soon afterwards in a riding accident.'

'How tragic! And her husband? Did he go on living here?'

'No. He sold up and went to live in Ireland. I suppose he wanted to get away from his unhappy memories. But why are we talking about this sad story? We're here to enjoy ourselves. What would you like for dessert?'

'Something creamy and wicked,' she replied.

He beckoned discreetly and a trolley was wheeled up for their inspection.

'This reminds me of the Viennese patisserie,' said Chloe.

She pointed to a confection of cream and strawberries.

Adam made his own choice and the trolley was wheeled away.

When Chloe finally laid down her fork, she gave a deep sigh of satisfaction.

'A wonderful meal,' agreed Adam. 'Would you like coffee now or later?'

'Later, please. I don't think I could manage even a coffee right now.'

'What about a stroll in the gardens then? The dancing doesn't start for,' he glanced at his watch, 'half an hour. It'll be nice and cool outside.'

'What a lovely idea.' Chloe stood up and Adam held her chair, looking at her dress admiringly.

'It's very pretty. The colour is perfect with your hair. An ice princess.'

'I hope I'm not as cold as an ice princess.'

'I'm sure you're not.' He gave her a deep and meaningful stare and Chloe felt a shiver of anticipation.

It was quite dark outside, but little lights illuminated the pathways. At first they walked side by side although not touching, then Adam put a hand lightly round her waist and pulled her close.

'I don't know whether it's the flowers I can smell or your perfume,' he said.

'I hope it's my perfume. It's very special.'

'And very appropriate. It's L'Heure Bleu, isn't it? The blue hour. The gardens have a blue haze over them and you are wearing a blue dress. Everything is just right.'

They strolled on slowly and stopped at a gently splashing fountain. Chloe thought she had never been so happy as she gazed into the water. When Adam slipped his arm round her again, she almost stopped breathing. Would he kiss her?

'If we want to dance, we must go in,' he said.

He led her away from the fountain and up the path towards the house.

Chloe couldn't trust herself to speak. Why hadn't he kissed her? There was no one around. His eyes had been full of admiration as he'd looked at her. Didn't he want to kiss her?

But she mustn't think about it, it would spoil the evening.

They walked up the steps to the terrace, through the glass doors and into the ballroom. Without a word, Adam took her in his arms and all her disappointment vanished. There were several more hours of the evening left. Anything might happen. She abandoned herself to the music and the dance.

'So didn't he kiss you at all?' asked Betty, who was obviously terribly disappointed in spite of all her warnings to her friend.

'Well . . . yes he did, sort of. We had another stroll around the gardens before the taxi came,' said Chloe, 'and we stopped in a rose arbour. The scent was fabulous. He put his arms round me and kissed me. Just once.'

'Was it a little peck or a deep, lingering, passionate kiss?' asked Betty.

'For goodness sake! You spend too much time at the pictures. It was just a kiss.'

But it wasn't just a kiss. Betty's description was accurate; it was long, lingering and passionate. A kiss to remember and treasure.

'I knew it,' said Betty. 'He's trifling with your affections.'

'It was only a friendly peck.' Chloe

protested. 'He wasn't pretending he loved me or anything like that.'

'We'll see,' said Betty. 'Now come on, it's time for church. Aunt Ellen's been ready for ages.'

She stopped in the doorway.

'And by the way, I won't be going to the pictures ever again. Rudolf Valentino is dead so *my* heart is broken!'

The whole of the next week, Adam was in London for a medical conference. Chloe hugged to herself the memory of the wonderful evening at The Belmont and the bliss of being held in Adam's arms. She longed for him to return.

The weather was fine and sunny, and on Saturday Chloe and Betty finished shopping and decided to treat themselves to an ice at a café that had a courtyard garden overlooking the river.

A flotilla of ducks were sailing up and down the water near the bank, and Chloe begged a bread roll from a waitress and threw small pieces to the ducklings.

'We don't need to worry about fitting into our evening dresses any more,' said Chloe, 'so we can have some really enormous ices.'

When the ice-cream dishes were

empty, Chloe sat back in her chair with a sigh of contentment.

'I like it here.' She looked around at the umbrella-topped tables, the flowers and the tranquil river. 'We must come again before the fine weather disappears.'

'Chloe! Betty!'

The voice came from somewhere behind them. Chloe froze. It couldn't be!

But it was! Making her way between the tables, red-gold curls shining in the sunshine, Susannah Blaine was trying to attract their attention.

'Oh, no!' muttered Betty.

'Hello, you two.' Susannah smiled happily, sure of a welcome. 'Can we join you? This is Paul.'

Betty recognised the young man who was supposed to have been Susannah's partner at the Charity Ball.

'Go and get some ices and a long cool drink, Paul,' ordered Susannah, and he went off without a word.

'He's a pet but a bit of a prune,' the

girl said unkindly. 'I like older men.' She sat back and smiled at Betty. 'You met him at the ball, didn't you? And how is your ankle?' she asked Chloe, without waiting for Betty to reply. 'Great shame you missed all the fun. Father tried to stop me going, but I can handle him.'

Chloe looked at her. The day's outing was spoilt. The person she least wanted to see had turned up.

'I thought you were in Scotland,' she said.

But Susannah didn't want to talk about her holiday. 'I was and now I'm back,' she said sharply. 'Did you see Adam Raven dancing with me at the ball?' she demanded as she turned towards Betty. 'We dance really well together. Well, we should. We've had quite a bit of practice lately.'

She leaned back in her chair and looked up into the branches above her.

'Dear Adam,' she said affectionately. 'We're so very fond of each other.'

Betty glanced at Chloe's face and stood up.

'I'm sorry, Susannah, but we'll have to go. I have a dental appointment in fifteen minutes.'

Susannah looked taken aback. 'On a Saturday afternoon?'

'Yes. My dentist works occasional Saturday afternoons. Come on, Chloe, we'll have to hurry.'

Gathering up their bags, they quickly left the restaurant.

Outside, Chloe gave her friend a despairing look.

'Oh, Betty! Susannah is quite determined. What hope do I have? He'll never love me if he has the chance of a catch like Susannah.'

On Sunday afternoon, there was a knock at the front door just as Chloe was coming down the stairs.

'I'll go,' she called to Nancy, the maid, who was hurrying to answer it.

'Chloe. Good afternoon. I'm so glad you're in. I . . . I wanted to speak to you.'

Adam Raven stood on the doorstep, twisting his hat between his hands.

She stood back, astonished but delighted, opening the door wider.

'Of course. Please come in.'

He hesitated.

'Actually, I wondered whether you would come for a walk with me? We could go to the park. It would be easier to talk there.'

Her heart began to beat faster. He wanted to talk to her alone? Why?

But no, it couldn't be that.

'Just let me get my hat. I won't be a moment.'

'I won't come in. I'll wait at the gate,' he said.

She collected her hat, started out of the front door, then remembered that Betty and Aunt Ellen were in the drawing-room.

She went back and popped her head into the room.

'I'm just going for a walk. Won't be long.'

She was gone before Betty could ask questions or offer to accompany her.

She and Adam crossed the road and walked towards the park gates at the end of the road.

'Have you had a nice weekend?' he asked her.

'Yes, thank you.'

She would forget Susannah's part in it.

'Lovely day.'

'Yes.' Chloe glanced at him. Surely he hadn't asked her to go for a walk so that he could discuss the weather.

They reached the park and turned in at the gates. Perhaps he'll say what he came to say now, thought Chloe. But they walked in silence for a few more minutes.

They reached a bench in the shade under a tree and Adam stopped.

'Shall we sit down?'

'I think I'd rather walk.'

'Oh . . . well.' They walked on. 'Let's go this way,' he said. 'It's quieter.'

'Adam.' She couldn't bear it any longer. She felt as if her heart would explode at any moment. She stopped and turned to him. 'Did you want to say something special to me?'

'Yes,' he said quietly. 'It's about the other evening. The evening we went to the Belmont.'

Her heart stopped pounding and began to sing.

'It was a lovely evening!' she said, turning towards him, eyes shining. 'I enjoyed it so much.'

'I know. And so did I. But I feel I must apologise.'

'Apologise? Whatever for?'

'I'm afraid I forgot myself. The wine, the evening, you looking so lovely in your blue dress — I got carried away. I shouldn't have kissed you.'

Chloe was confused. What was this? What was he trying to say? Certainly not what she'd been expecting him to say, that was for sure. She began to feel rather foolish.

'But, Adam, what's a kiss? We'd just spent an enjoyable evening together. You were just being . . . ' she hesitated ' . . . friendly.'

It sounded silly even to her.

'I was not being friendly, and from your response, I think you felt it meant something more than friendship too.'

Chloe blushed and turned away so that he shouldn't see her face.

'Chloe, a kiss like that is almost a commitment, a declaration. And I'm not in a position to commit myself to anyone. My career has to come first. I must work my way up, become financially secure before I can offer a girl anything. I admit I'm very attracted to you, but I had no right to kiss you like that. Will you accept my apology?'

She was silent for a long time.

He looked at her anxiously.

'Chloe?'

'I wish you hadn't said all this, Adam. You've spoilt my memories of a lovely evening. I didn't mind your kiss; in fact, I enjoyed it. As for commitment, I didn't expect any. But I thought we were friends.'

He reached for her hand but she pulled away.

'Please take me home, Adam. I think we've said all we have to say.'

'Chloe, don't be angry. I just wanted to make the situation clear. I didn't want to deceive you, to let you believe . . . '

'That you were attracted to me? Thank you, Adam, the situation is quite clear now and the last thing I would want is to be a hindrance to you in your career.' She turned away. 'At least

Susannah Blaine and her father will be happy.'

She started to walk back towards the gate, hardly able to believe that she'd made that remark.

'Chloe!' He hurried after her, put his hands on her shoulders and spun her round to face him. 'What do you mean?'

'I should think that's obvious. Everyone knows that Dr Blaine's daughter is a special friend of yours.'

He stared at her in silence for a few seconds. Then he dropped his hands.

'Is that what you believe? That I'm interested in Susannah Blaine because of who her father is? Because I want to marry my boss's daughter?'

Chloe faced him in silence.

He gave a deep sigh.

'Dr Blaine is concerned about Susannah's choice of male companions. She's a flighty girl, and headstrong. I admit that he has asked me to partner her on certain social occasions so that she doesn't choose a completely unsuitable escort for herself. And yes, I admit that I do as he asks because he can influence my future career. But I assure you, I have no romantic interest whatever in Susannah Blaine.'

Chloe looked at him, tears beginning to prick the back of her eyelids. If this was true, he should now say that he preferred her. Even that he loved her. She waited, but he said nothing more.

'Please take me home,' she said again.

They walked back to the house in silence.

They reached the gate and he raised his hat to her. 'I'll see you at the surgery tomorrow,' he said and was gone.

Chloe walked slowly round the house to the garden where, enveloped in a cloud of misery, she sat down on the old swing that hung from a sturdy branch of an oak tree.

She could hardly bear to think of the past half-hour. But, to be fair to Adam, it was all her own fault. He had been kind and considerate, taking her out because she had missed an evening to which she'd been looking forward. If she had read more into his behaviour than he had meant, then it was not his fault.

Lost in her thoughts, she sat gently swinging to and fro until she was startled to hear Betty's voice calling her from the terrace.

'Chloe! Tea! Are you coming in?'

Chloe waved her straw hat in acknowledgement.

She would tell Betty about this afternoon, but not yet.

After tea, Chloe asked Betty if she would help her to pin up the hem of her new woollen dress, which she had by now almost finished making.

'This is going to look really nice,' said Betty through a mouthful of pins. 'If I buy some material, will you help me make a dress? I'm not very good at sewing.'

'Of course. You know I will.'

'There.' Betty inserted the last pin. 'Finished. Are you going to sew it now?'

'I think so. Might as well finish it.'

'Shall I stay and talk to you?' The two girls were upstairs in Chloe's bedroom and Betty didn't wait for an answer but climbed on to Chloe's bed and made herself comfortable.

'Where did you go with Adam?'

'How do you know I went out with Adam?'

'Aunt Ellen and I saw him walking down the path. And you said you were going for a walk.'

'A female detective!'

'Well? Where did you go?'

'Just to the park.'

Chloe threaded a needle and began to stitch the hem.

'What did he he want?'

'He wanted to apologise for kissing me when he took me out to The Belmont last weekend.'

'What? Men don't apologise to girls for kissing them!'

'Adam did. He thought I might see it as a commitment and he's not able to make a commitment to any girl yet until he's established in his career.'

There was silence for a while then Betty said, 'Did he mention Susannah?'

'Not until I asked him about her. He admitted that he escorts her to please Dr Blaine but he says he has no romantic interest in her.'

'But you don't believe him?'

The face Chloe turned towards her was a mask of misery. 'I don't know, Betty. He takes me out but he also takes Susannah out. He says he doesn't love her but he doesn't say he loves me. And yet the way he kissed me!'

Betty looked at her friend. 'It wasn't just a little peck, then, after all?'

Chloe looked shamefaced.

'Chloe, if I show you something, will you promise not to get angry?'

'What do you mean?'

Betty swung her legs off the bed and left the room.

When she returned she was holding a magazine. She dropped it on to the bed. It was a nursing magazine, folded back at the situations vacant page. She had marked an advertisement at the bottom: '*Nurse-companion wanted for elderly lady in beautiful house in the Cotswolds.*'

Chloe read the words twice then looked at her friend.

'So?'

'Perhaps you need to get away from Adam.'

Chloe pushed away the magazine and stood up.

'You're not angry?' Betty looked at her anxiously.

'I've just remembered I promised to help Aunt Ellen with a jigsaw. Excuse me, please.'

Chloe was quiet during dinner and Betty felt sure that her friend was furious with her over the advertisement.

But when Aunt Ellen disappeared to discuss some linen repairs with the maid, Chloe produced the magazine.

'When you showed me this, I did feel cross,' she admitted. 'You seemed to be pushing me into going away. But I've been doing some serious thinking.'

'I don't see how I can possibly carry on working with Adam when I feel the way I do about him. I love him, Betty, truly I do, and I can't believe that he feels nothing for me. But if he'd rather break my heart than fall out of favour with Dr Blaine then I think I'm better off without him.'

'You were right all along. I should have kept my distance from him from the start.'

'So are you going to apply for that position as nurse-companion?'

'Yes. I know the Cotswolds slightly. It's a very beautiful area. I shall write a letter of application straight away, but no one must know. Please say nothing to anyone. If I'm successful, there will be time enough to decide what to say to Adam and to Dr Blaine.'

A week later, a thick cream envelope dropped through the letter box. Betty's heart sank as she picked it up and looked at the postmark.

'Chloe,' she called up the stairs. 'There's a letter for you.'

The letter invited Chloe to an interview at the Avon Court Hotel in London to meet Olivia Keeling, the daughter of her prospective new employer.

'I wonder why she wants to meet you in London?' Betty mused.

The two girls had gone out into the garden and were sitting in the shade of a huge oak tree, drinking tea.

'Probably she doesn't live with her mother,' said Chloe. 'I expect the next interview — if I have one — will be with Mrs Keeling at her home.'

'Are you sure about this?' asked Betty, reaching out and squeezing her friend's hand. 'If you're offered the job it will mean living in a new home with strangers.'

Chloe considered.

'No, I'm not sure. I have a lot of doubts. And I shall miss you dreadfully. But underneath, I'm quite excited. Anyway, I might not get the job.'

'I think you will,' Betty prophesied. 'But you need to be quite sure that it's what you want before you accept it.'

'If it's offered, I shall take it,' said Chloe in a firm voice.

'Would you like me to come with you to London?'

'Oh, Betty, would you? I'm not worried about the interview, but it would be so nice to have someone to travel with me.'

'Of course I'll come. And when you've had your interview we can visit some of the big shops. We'll have a lovely day out!'

# Adam Says Goodbye

Chloe and Betty were in quite different frames of mind as they travelled down to London on the train.

Betty was excited at the prospect of a day in the city.

Chloe felt she was being torn two ways.

Part of her wanted to stay at the surgery in a job she knew she was good at and that she enjoyed — and with the possibility of a closer relationship with Adam, although she knew that was a remote hope.

But the thought of a new venture stirred her and she hoped that by putting distance between herself and Adam Raven, she would soon be able to forget him.

Olivia Keeling was tall and elegant but friendly, and Chloe felt relaxed with her at once.

They met in a little sitting-room which led off from Olivia's office.

'I work here at the hotel,' she explained. 'I arrange events — exhibitions, conferences and so on. I'm not able to get back to the Cotswolds as often as I would like, so it is essential that my mother has a constant companion who she likes and on whom she — and I — can rely.'

They settled down to discuss Chloe's qualifications for the job. Over coffee they talked of Chloe's childhood, her training, and her present duties at the surgery.

Olivia offered her a plate of delicious caramel biscuits and smiled apologetically.

'May I ask why you want to leave your present position?'

Chloe was conscious that she had to give a truthful answer, but she didn't want to discuss her private feelings with someone she'd just met, however sympathetic.

She made the conventional excuse of

wanting a change of scenery, saying that the prospect of working in such a beautiful part of England was an attraction, and making the vaguest reference to personal reasons.

Olivia's cool grey eyes studied her keenly, but she didn't press for more details.

At last she stood up and gave Chloe a charming smile.

'Thank you for your interest in the position, Miss Perle. I have two more girls to see, but I promise to be in touch within the next few days.'

Chloe joined Betty downstairs in the lounge with a relieved expression on her face.

'Well?' Betty asked eagerly.

'I don't know yet but I feel quite confident.'

Betty indicated the coffee pot in front of her, but Chloe shook her head.

'No, thank you. I've had enough coffee. What I need now is some fresh air.'

'Just tell me this, what sort of job is it?'

'Miss Keeling said she wouldn't go into too many details yet, but that if I had a second interview it would be at the house in the Cotswolds and then I could see for myself. She did say that her mother had had two heart attacks and needed some nursing care, although she isn't an invalid.'

'Right.' Betty stood up. 'Now you're going to put it out of your mind and we're going shopping. We can get a cab outside the hotel. A few minutes' drive and we'll be in the centre of everything.'

To the amusement of a passing waiter, she executed a few Charleston steps and danced towards the door singing, 'When the red, red robin comes bob, bob, bobbin' along.'

Chloe, laughing helplessly, followed in her wake.

★   ★   ★

The rest of the day passed in a whirl. They darted up and down arcades and in and out of shops. Chloe began to

110

worry that they would never find their way back to the station and their train home.

'I wonder whether I should buy some new clothes while we're here, just in case I do get the job?' she asked. 'Do you think the Keelings will be very grand? Will they dress for dinner every night?'

'I shouldn't worry, you'll probably take your meals in the servants' hall,' teased Betty.

'I don't think they'll be that grand, and it is the country, after all. Things may be more relaxed there. But I could get some long skirts and perhaps some dressy blouses. What do you think?'

'I think you'd be as well to treat yourself while you're here, and I think perhaps I'll have a look for something nice for myself, too. Goodness knows when we might get the chance to come through to London again.'

They had reached the top of some steep narrow stairs into the dress department of a large store.

'I'll have a look around here. For a black skirt and perhaps a contrast.'

'No.' Betty was firm. 'Not black, it's too conventional. Deep blue, almost navy. Let's see if they have anything.'

In the end, Chloe left the department store with two skirts; one midnight blue, one deep rose. She was very pleased with them.

On the way out, in the hat department, she grabbed her friend's arm.

'Betty — look! I simply must try it.' She pointed to a small cream cloche hat trimmed with a deep chocolate brown ribbon and tiny gold and brown roses.

In due course the box containing the hat was added to her collection of parcels and they left the shop giggling.

Betty remembered seeing a small café tucked away in a side street, where she hoped they could get some lunch.

They managed to find their way back to it and settled themselves into a corner.

Chloe was surprised to discover that she was quite hungry.

'Shopping is hungry work,' agreed her friend.

When, refreshed, they left the café, an open-topped bus went by with a sign on the side — *London Tours*.

'Oh!' Chloe said. 'We always promised ourselves a ride on one of those when we worked in London, but we never got round to it. Have we time now, do you think?'

But Betty hurried her on. 'We're not here to see the sights, we're here to go shopping, remember? And I haven't bought anything for myself yet.'

Chloe was instantly contrite. 'I'm sorry. I didn't think. Let's get some things for you now. What would you like?'

Betty bought, in quick succession, a handbag, a pair of shoes, and two smart jackets.

They were looking up at Big Ben when Betty noticed how late it was getting.

'We'd better get a cab to the station or we'll miss the train,' said Chloe. 'I should think we've just about enough money between us for the fare.'

It wasn't many days later that Chloe was invited to her second interview which was to take place at The Keelings' house in the Cotswolds.

She was invited to arrive during Saturday and to stay until after lunch on Sunday. Olivia Keeling thought that would give both her mother and Chloe time enough to decide whether they liked each other, and for Chloe to decide whether life in such a quiet part of England would suit her.

Chloe hummed to herself as the train approached Evesham and the fruit-growing area of the Midlands. Fruit trees marched across the horizon like ranks of soldiers. Neatly planted rows of vegetables stretched into the distance. Groups of people were busy in the fields filling baskets with plums and strawberries. A few stopped to stretch obviously aching backs and waved at the train.

Amused, Chloe waved back.

The train left Evesham and moved on, across a countryside thick with smallholdings, towards Cheston Parva, the track running parallel to the road.

The train pulled into Bayton Green Station and, gathering her small suitcase and handbag, Chloe descended to the platform and looked around.

She knew she would be met but was surprised to see Olivia herself waving to her. She had expected a chauffeur or a taxi driver.

'Miss Perle!' Miss Keeling hurried towards her and shook her hand. 'Did you have a good journey? The car's this way.'

Chloe tried not to let it show that she was surprised at Miss Keeling being a motorist. She was a career woman, living in London, so Chloe supposed it was to be expected.

'This is my brother's car,' explained Miss Keeling. 'I have my own car in

London, but it's much smaller. I use the train to travel back and forth.'

Chloe settled herself in the big open-topped tourer. It was very comfortable and she tried to look as if she was used to travelling in such style.

They left the station and set off towards Cheston Parva, passing fields of vegetables and fruit trees. Here and there along the roadside, local produce was advertised for sale from ramshackle wooden huts and stalls.

'We grow our own,' said Miss Keeling nodding towards the stalls. 'We have a huge garden and a wonderful gardener.'

They entered Broadway, one of the most famous of the Cotswold villages which, as it was Saturday, was quite crowded with visitors.

As they drove along the main street with its green-verged pavements and old, spreading trees, Chloe was fascinated by the pretty cottages built of golden stone with their dormer windows in their steep roofs and bow windows on to the street.

Beyond the village of Broadway, they climbed the incredibly steep Fish Hill and passed the entrance to Broadway Tower, which could be seen from miles away.

Miss Keeling had told her that Hampdens, her mother's house, was on the edge of the next village, Cheston Parva.

Soon, they passed a signpost that pointed the way to Cheston Parva and Chloe began to look eagerly around her.

The road, with the trees meeting overhead to form welcome shade, began to descend to the outskirts of the village. Here, too, the houses were made of golden Cotswold stone, but each stood at an angle to the others in its own flower-filled garden. Low, uneven stone walls topped with shaggy green hedges surrounded the gardens.

They hadn't driven much further when Miss Keeling suddenly slowed the car.

'Here we are.'

Chloe eagerly studied the house which was called Hampdens. It was bigger than its neighbours and looking as if it had stood unchanged for hundreds of years.

Olivia stopped the car and they both sat gazing at the timeless building with its weathered stonework and picturesque uneven roof.

'It's beautiful.' Chloe was enraptured.

Miss Keeling looked at her and smiled.

'It is,' she agreed.

Hampdens was built of golden-yellow limestone, but time had weathered it to a rich, dull cream. The old, wooden front door was set deep into a pillared porch and the upstairs windows were small-paned dormers set into the grey slate roof. The rest of the windows were tall and large-paned, separated by stone mullions and swathed in berried foliage.

Chloe imagined herself sitting with easel and paints on the grass verge.

What a lovely picture the house would make. But she was no artist. Perhaps it would be better to try a little pencil sketch to give Betty some idea of the beauty of the house.

Miss Keeling started the engine again and drove a few yards down the narrow lane to the left of the house and through the wide entrance to a courtyard.

They climbed out.

'Leave your case — we'll get it later. Come and meet Mrs Foster, our housekeeper.'

She led Chloe into an old-fashioned kitchen with a big range against one wall, and a scrubbed table in the centre of the room. The smell of newly-baked cakes scented the air.

Mrs Foster, a tall, angular woman in a flowered overall, shook Chloe's hand.

'You're just in time for a cup of tea and a maid-of-honour cake.' She smiled. 'Come and sit down.'

Chloe was surprised, but happy to do so. She was ready for a cup of tea after her journey. She had expected a more formal introduction to the household, but she took off her hat and sat where Mrs Foster indicated.

Miss Keeling joined them at the table.

'We all gravitate to the kitchen when Mrs Foster is baking. Cakes taste better fresh from the oven than eaten when we're sitting in state in the drawing-room.'

The little cake was delicious and Chloe happily accepted another.

'I love almond flavours,' she said. 'These are wonderful.'

'When you've had your tea I'll show you to your room. My mother is resting at the moment,' Miss Keeling explained. 'But by the time you've settled in she should be awake and ready to meet you.'

Chloe's room was fresh and bright and the walls were white to reflect every bit of light that the tiny windows let in. The sky-blue curtains and bedspread were splashed with white and yellow daisies. A comfortable old armchair filled with yellow cushions stood next to the bed and there were yellow rugs to match on the wooden floor.

'What a lovely, sunny room.' Chloe crossed to the window. 'Oh, and a beautiful garden. I didn't realise it was so large.'

'I miss it when I'm in London,' said Miss Keeling. 'Mother used to do a lot of gardening but, of course, now she can only sit and watch. But as I said, we have an excellent gardener.'

Chloe looked out of the window again. She could see the narrow lane at the side of the house, winding away round a bend.

'I'll leave you for ten minutes,' said Miss Keeling, 'then I'll send for you.'

There was a little hand basin behind a screen in the corner. Chloe washed her hands and glanced at her reflection. Her face was pink from the sun. She tried to tone it down with her powder puff but it made little difference, and unpacking would have to wait till later;

she could hear footsteps on the stairs.

'Have you everything you want, Miss?' It was Mrs Foster. 'I've come to take you down to the drawing-room. Mrs Keeling is ready to see you.'

Chloe followed her down the polished wooden stairs.

'Hold the rail until you're used to them,' Mrs Foster advised.

If Chloe had been asked to guess what the Keelings' drawing-room in the old house would be like, she would have described exactly the room she now entered.

She had an impression of deep chairs, upholstered in soft, faded flower colours, dark polished wood, and bright copper reflecting the dancing flames of the log fire. The room was large and cool, and even on this late summer day, Mrs Keeling, who sat on a day-bed in the window overlooking the garden, obviously needed the warmth of a fire.

Her daughter came to the door to meet Chloe and took her across the room to introduce her to her mother.

'Come and sit beside me, Chloe.' Mrs Keeling patted a stool next to the day-bed. 'Chloe Perle! What a lovely name. And doesn't it suit you!'

She studied Chloe in silence for a few seconds.

'Forgive me, my dear, but I don't believe I've ever seen anyone so fair. How would you describe your hair? Silver-gilt, I think,' she went on without waiting for Chloe's reply. 'And your skin is so pale and beautiful. Perle is a good name for you; you look like a pearl.'

Chloe began to blush and Olivia Keeling came to her aid.

'You're embarrassing Miss Perle, Mother.'

Instantly the old lady took Chloe's hand. 'I'm sorry, my dear, but I admire beauty when I see it. Now then, I can't call you Miss Perle. It's too formal.'

'Chloe, then, please.'

Chloe looked at the small figure with the fine-boned face and neat, grey hair brushed across her forehead. She must expect straight talking from this self-assured elderly lady. But she liked her at first glance. She was sure they could be happy together.

'Off you go, Olivia. I'm sure you have things to do. Chloe and I have lots to discuss.'

For an hour, Chloe and Mrs Keeling chatted happily and the girl felt all her nervousness vanish as they talked.

'We dine at seven,' the elderly lady said at last. 'I don't like to eat late. It's six now, so perhaps you'd like to go and get changed?'

Chloe returned to her room and sat down to think for a moment in the armchair by the bed. She liked Mrs Keeling and her daughter; Mrs Foster was very pleasant; the house and its setting were perfect — so was there anything that would make her hesitate to take the job if it was offered?

She knew the answer — Adam!

She leaned back in the chair and closed her eyes. Was she doing the right thing, running away from Alderton and burying herself in a Cotswold village? But Adam had made it plain that he didn't view Chloe as a romantic prospect. Not while he still needed to make a good impression on his employer.

She pictured his face. Thick brown hair, green eyes under heavy brows and a solemn expression which could break into the most appealing smile.

A sudden realisation that time was passing sent her springing out of the armchair and reaching for her suitcase. She had only twenty minutes to get ready for dinner. She would have to hurry. Decisions about the future would have to wait.

★   ★   ★

Mrs Keeling and Olivia had changed into simple evening clothes and Chloe was glad that she'd packed her new, midnight-blue evening skirt and a white silk blouse. The ladies nodded with approval as she entered the dining-room.

Mrs Foster had prepared an enjoyable meal of roast chicken with tiny potatoes, peas and baby carrots.

'From our own garden,' said Mrs Keeling with pride. 'We're self-sufficient in vegetables. Rosalyn's such a good gardener.'

'Rosalyn?' Chloe's head jerked up in surprise.

'She's Mrs Foster's daughter,' explained Mrs Keeling. 'You'll meet her if you wander round the garden tomorrow.'

'And tomorrow, you'll meet the other member of the family,' said Olivia. 'My brother, Benedict.'

'This is not a completely female household,' said Mrs Keeling. 'Benedict lives here with us but he's in France at the moment. He's an artist.'

Perhaps Benedict has the final say in my appointment, thought Chloe. After all, we'd have to live in such close proximity. I wonder what he's like?

The next morning, Mrs Keeling had breakfast in her room and Chloe ate with Olivia downstairs.

'I'm going to get Mother ready for the day,' said Olivia when they had finished. 'Would you like to have a walk round the garden? Benedict came back late last night. You might bump into him. He does a lot of sketching out there.'

But the first person Chloe met on her walk was a hefty young woman in trousers, boots, and a check shirt, who was vigorously weeding a vegetable patch.

She seemed engrossed in the task but looked up and smiled pleasantly as Chloe approached.

'Hello. Can I help you? You're visiting here, aren't you?'

'I am, but I hope I might be living

here soon,' Chloe found herself saying, and realised she meant it. A night's sleep seemed to have sorted out her intentions. 'I'm Chloe Perle. I might be coming to work here as Mrs Keeling's nurse-companion.'

Rosalyn got to her feet and held out a hand, first rubbing it clean on her trousers.

'Rosalyn Foster. I'm the gardener, as you can see.'

'We ate some of your produce at dinner last night. It was very good.'

'Thanks.' Rosalyn looked around. 'Do you want a tour or would you prefer to walk round on your own?'

'I think I'd better stay near the house in case they call me. But I'd love a proper tour some time.'

'Right you are!'

Rosalyn returned to her weeding and Chloe wandered down a paved path that led towards a fountain that stood in the centre of an ornamental pool.

'My goodness me! I do believe I can see a fairy,' said a voice.

Chloe looked around but could see no one.

'A fairy in an ice-blue dress with beautiful silver hair,' went on the definitely masculine voice.

She walked round to the other side of the pool to see a low stone bench and seated upon it was a young man about five years older than herself. He had a sketchpad on his knees and stood up as she approached.

'Benedict Keeling.' He held out a hand. 'You're Chloe Perle and you've come to see if you can bear to take on my dear Mama.'

Chloe studied him. She wasn't sure she liked this flippant young man, but he was certainly good to look at with his long pale face and long dark hair.

'Mrs Keeling seems a charming lady,' she said. 'We seem to get on very well.'

'I'm sure you do. She's already told me she likes you very much.'

Chloe looked up to see Olivia waving to her from the far side of the pond.

'I think your sister wants me,' she

said. 'I must go.'

'Wait! Would you pose for me?'

Startled, Chloe felt her face go pink. Pose? For an artist?

'Oh, I don't think . . . ' she began. 'Look, I really must go.'

Olivia was waiting for her. 'You found Benedict then? You look rather bothered. Is anything wrong?'

'Well,' Chloe wasn't sure what to say. 'He asked me if I would pose for him.'

'Oh, dear. And you feel embarrassed by the idea! Well, don't be! Benedict isn't that kind of artist! He's an illustrator. Of children's books,' she added.

'Oh.' Chloe felt both awkward and relieved.

They reached the house and Olivia took her to Mrs Keeling.

The older woman greeted her enthusiastically. 'Chloe. Did you have a good night? Sit down, my dear, and we'll talk some more.'

'And she certainly can talk,' Chloe told Betty at home, later that night.

'She's a real chatterbox, but so nice and friendly.'

'So you've got the job?'

'Yes. After lunch we all sat over coffee and Olivia said they'd decided I was just what they were looking for.'

'And you said . . . ?'

'I said yes. I'm sure I shall be happy there. But tomorrow I'll have to tell Adam and Dr Blaine.'

'Dr Blaine first,' advised Betty. 'He mustn't hear it from anyone else.'

Chloe stared thoughtfully into her cocoa.

'You're right. I'll tell him tomorrow.'

She was unable, in any case, to talk to Adam that Monday morning because he was away from the surgery all day and not expected back until late afternoon.

'You haven't been with us long. You have another position?' Dr Blaine barked at her when she explained that she would like to leave as soon as it was convenient.

She hesitated. It wasn't in her nature to lie but she didn't want to let Adam know where she was going.

She prevaricated.

'I want to go home for a while,' she said.

'Can I help with anything?' Dr Blaine's voice was more kindly. 'You have problems at home?'

'No. I can cope. Thank you. But I would like to leave soon.'

He looked down at his desk and sighed.

'Very well. If I can arrange an agency nurse temporarily, you can go at the end of the week. Will that do?'

She thanked him and escaped to the treatment room.

This was going to be difficult. Other members of the staff would want to know why she was leaving. She hadn't been in the job all that long. She'd have to tell the same story; that she was going home for a few weeks.

She heard footsteps in the corridor and the sound of a key in a lock. She peeped out. Adam! Checking her appearance in the mirror she took a deep breath and walked quickly down the corridor to his room.

'Chloe! I thought you'd have left an hour ago. Why are you still here?'

'I have to speak to you. It's important.'

'Yes?'

'I'm leaving here,' she blurted out.

'Leaving? But where are you going? And why?'

'I just need to get away from here.'

'Away from here or away from me?' he asked her, frowning.

Chloe looked out of the window, biting her lip.

'It's not still that idea you've got into your head about Susannah Blaine, is it? I thought I'd explained that. Don't you believe me?' His voice was low but

133

agitated. 'I'm not in a position to commit myself to anyone at the moment. If I was . . . ' He took a deep breath. 'If I was, there's no one I'd prefer but you.'

She looked at him with a flash of anger. 'Oh! I see! So I'm to stay here pretending that we feel nothing more than friendship for each other, and hang around in the background while you toady up to Dr Blaine and pay court to his daughter?'

'It does sound dreadful when you put it like that.'

'Well, how else would you put it?' She glared at him. If only he would say that he loved her. If only he would take her in his arms and give her a kiss that needed no apology because he meant it.

She waited. Just three words and a kiss and she would give up her Cotswold dream.

She moved towards the door. 'I'm leaving on Friday.'

'Very well, you seem to have made up your mind.' He turned to the desk and picked up a folder. 'Goodbye, Chloe. I wish you nothing but the best for the future,' he said, without looking round.

Chloe stumbled from the room without another word.

# Chloe Settles In

'Chloe, dear, Mrs Graham has come for a chat about the Mothers' Union supper, so I shall be busy for an hour.' Mrs Keeling settled herself on the day-bed. 'Would you be so kind as to take these letters to Benedict? And don't rush back. I'm sure he'll want to show you his studio and his drawings.'

Chloe smiled at Mrs Graham as she passed her in the hall on her way to the kitchen.

'Mrs Foster, how do I get to Benedict's studio? Mrs Keeling has asked me to take him his post.'

As usual, the kitchen was full of wonderful cooking smells. Mrs Foster took a tray of biscuits from the oven.

'You can take some of these up to Mr Benedict.' Mrs Foster laughed. 'He loves my homemade biscuits.' She slid several on to a plate. 'They'll soon cool and go crisp.'

She led Chloe to a door at the back of the kitchen. It opened on to a covered way.

'Go to the end,' Mrs Foster told her, pointing to the right, 'and up the stairs.'

The covered way ran the length of the courtyard at the back of the garages. Iron spiral stairs ended at a big black door.

Chloe climbed the stairs and knocked on the door.

'Come in.' The voice was faint.

Timidly she pushed open the door and stared in amazement. The studio seemed to stretch away into the distance. No wonder Benedict's voice sounded faint. He was sitting in a rocking chair looking out of a picture window at the far end.

'What a huge room,' she said.

'Jolly cold in the winter.' He got out of the chair and came to meet her. 'It's impossible to heat. What have we here?'

'Your post and Mrs Foster's biscuits.'

'Come and sit down. I'll make some coffee to go with them. Can you stay?'

'Mrs Keeling said she would be all right for an hour.'

'Wonderful. Coffee coming up. Then I'll show you around.'

As she waited for her coffee, Chloe examined her surroundings. The room was large, but Benedict had somehow managed to fill it with his materials and his artwork.

There were several huge sloping tables covered with sketches. Two easels near the window bore half-finished oil paintings. Propped against every wall were canvases, and tables and shelves held paints, pots of brushes and the assorted clutter of an artist's studio.

In the roof, huge windows let in the maximum amount of daylight and, Chloe supposed, contributed to the cold atmosphere when there was no sun.

Benedict had been busy at the table in the corner. Now he appeared at her side bearing two mugs of coffee.

'You do take milk?' he asked her, looking at her quizzically.

'Yes, please, but no sugar.'

Chloe sat in the rocking chair; Benedict pulled up a stool and sat opposite her.

They sipped their coffee.

'Well, how has your first week been?' he asked.

'I love it here. I know I shall be happy.'

'No regrets at leaving your other life?'

Chloe looked into her coffee cup. 'No. No regrets.'

'It must seem very quiet after a busy doctors' practice.'

'That's what makes it such a change. And I love the peace of the country-side.'

'You might not be so keen to come next summer when the visitors descend in droves. Charabancs and cars everywhere.'

Chloe drank her coffee and didn't answer. Next summer was a long way away. For now, she was taking each day as it came.

She accepted another biscuit.

'Mrs Foster is a wonderful cook. I hope I don't put on lots of weight.'

'Mama will keep you running around. You won't have time to get fat. Now, let me show you my studio.'

On the opposite wall a noticeboard was covered with brightly-coloured dust covers for children's books.

Chloe read the titles out loud.

''*Milly Moppet Goes to the Seaside.*' '*Milly Moppet on the Farm.*' '*Milly Moppet has a Tea Party.*'' She pointed to the last book cover. 'I know that one, I bought it for a friend's little girl last year. The pictures are lovely. Oh, aren't I silly! '*Pictures by Benedict Keeling*',' she said. 'Of course, I didn't connect the name.' She turned to smile at Benedict. 'You're very talented.'

He bowed. 'Thank you, ma'am. But I only do the illustrations. A friend of mine writes the stories.'

Chloe looked again at the covers. ''*Story by Annabel Larne*',' she read. 'Have you worked together for long?'

'Several years. We only do Milly Moppet books together. I illustrate for other writers but she's a special friend.'

Annabel Larne, thought Chloe, visualising someone glamorous, probably tall and willowy with black hair and blue eyes. She wondered whether she would ever meet her.

Benedict began a conducted tour of the studio, holding out a drawing here and lifting up a canvas there. So many of them showed a winsome little girl with large dark eyes and dark hair drawn to each side, like window curtains, and tied with coloured ribbons above her ears.

'Milly Moppet.' Chloe smiled. 'Isn't she cute? Who is your model?'

Benedict bent over a table and began to sort some drawings.

'I don't believe she's just a product of your imagination,' persisted Chloe. 'She's so real.'

Benedict held out a small pile of sketches.

'These might interest you. Preliminary sketches for a fairy-story book.'

Chloe looked at him curiously, but his face was turned away from her and she couldn't see his expression. Why hadn't he answered her questions about his model? He must have heard her.

She looked at the fairy pictures.

'Why, these are exquisite!'

'I need to do several more. When I asked you to pose for me, these are what I had in mind. I still haven't done the fairy queen.'

'You want me for a fairy queen?' She began to laugh.

'What's so funny?'

'If you'd asked me ten years ago, I think I would have fainted with pleasure. Now . . . '

'Now?'

'It seems a bit — well — silly. Oh, not the drawings, of course, but the idea of a grown woman . . . '

'Please say yes.'

She looked at his sensitive face that

studied her so earnestly, and weakened.

'Well, if you're sure you need me.'

His face lit up.

'Wonderful. If we have a sunny day next week, we'll make a start.'

'Why do we need a sunny day?'

'It will be warmer in the garden in the sunshine.'

'In the garden? I thought you meant in the studio. What if anyone sees me? I take it you'll want me to dress up as a fairy?'

She began to regret her decision. The whole thing was beginning to sound a bit ridiculous. After all, she was a nurse, not an actress.

He put a hand on her arm.

'Don't worry. We have a lovely little secluded place in the garden. And we'll take Mama as a chaperone. She'll enjoy it. Thank you, Chloe.'

He gave her a beautiful, gentle smile. The flippancy of their first meeting had gone. Perhaps it had been due to nervousness, she decided.

Then she became aware of how long

she'd been in the studio. She glanced at her watch.

'Goodness, it's half-past. I must dash.'

He stood at the back door to watch her as she first made her way down the stairs and then flew along the covered way.

Then he went back into the studio and closed the door, a thoughtful expression on his face.

Olivia arrived at the house after breakfast next morning and greeted Chloe warmly. Chloe was pleased to see her. She liked this elegant, sophisticated woman who was never too busy to be concerned about her mother.

She answered Olivia's questions about her mother's welfare and they went together to see Mrs Keeling.

'Darling!' Mrs Keeling received her daughter's kiss on the cheek. 'This is a lovely surprise. How long can you stay?'

'Just until tomorrow after lunch. Now then, how are you two getting on?'

Mrs Keeling reached for Chloe's hand and patted it.

'She's a darling girl. You've found a treasure to take care of me. Benedict thinks so, too, don't you, my love?'

Benedict had entered the room as she was speaking.

'If Olivia is spending today with you, Mother, then can I take your treasure out for a few hours?'

Chloe glanced at him in surprise.

'I'm off to visit Annabel Larne,' he explained, 'the author of the Milly Moppet books. Would you like to come with me, Chloe?' he asked without waiting for his mother's answer.

Chloe looked to the other two women for permission.

'Go along, my dear. Have a break from this house. You'll love Annabel.'

Half an hour later, Chloe, in a turquoise-blue dress and hat, was with Benedict in his car speeding through the lanes away from Hampdens.

From time to time, Benedict smiled across at her.

'Not far. Annabel lives in a little village on the far side of Cheston Parva. We won't stay long. Then I can show you the place that I intend to use for your fairy castle.'

Annabel's cottage when they reached it was built of the ubiquitous golden

Cotswold stone but its roof was unusual. Tiny windows peeped beneath a deep thatch. The small garden was a riot of late summer flowers.

'I've never been inside a thatched cottage,' Chloe exclaimed in delight.

'It's very old. Annabel inherited it from her grandmother.'

The sound of yapping greeted them as Benedict knocked on the door.

'I hope you're not afraid of large, ferocious animals,' he said, as the door opened and a tiny old lady peeped out. She was smartly dressed and carefully coiffeured with just a touch of lipstick.

The grandmother, thought Chloe. She must live with Annabel.

'Annabel!' Benedict stepped forward and hugged the old lady. 'I've brought you a visitor.'

Annabel studied Chloe and seemed to like what she saw.

'Come in. Come in. You're just in time for elevenses.'

She opened a door and two tiny dogs shot out, yapping furiously.

Ignoring Chloe, they flung themselves at Benedict, bouncing around him on their little back legs like toys on elastic.

He bent and scooped them up and held one under each arm.

'Meet Bubble and Squeak,' he said to Chloe, 'two of my best friends.'

They licked his face energetically with tiny pink tongues.

Chloe was too captivated by the Yorkshire terriers to marvel that this little old lady was the imagined glamorous Annabel.

The cottage was small and cosy and seemed to be full of flowers — flowery cushions and curtains, a flowery carpet, and bowls of flowers on every surface.

Chloe was amused to see that even the tray and the coffee cups were decorated with painted roses.

A desk in the window overlooking the small garden was evidently Annabel's place of work. She took some papers from the desk and handed them to Benedict.

148

'I've been waiting for this,' he said to Chloe. 'Milly Moppet's latest adventure. '*Milly Moppet has a Birthday*'.'

He read in silence while Bubble and Squeak transferred their attentions to Chloe. They each presented her with a soft ball and she was kept busy rolling them for first one little dog and then the other.

Annabel watched the game.

'You're favoured,' she said. 'They don't always take to strangers. But, of course, you came with Benedict and they adore him.'

'Do you use them in your stories?' Chloe asked.

'They are going to have to have a series of their own,' the old lady said proudly. 'The first volume will be in the shops at Christmas.'

'How exciting. I love your Milly Moppet books.'

Annabel thanked her and passed a plate of buttered scones.

'Of course, the pictures make the story,' she said. 'Milly Moppet is so appealing in Benedict's illustrations. Are you an artist too?'

'No. I'm Mrs Keeling's new nurse-companion. Benedict is giving me a few hours away from work.'

They chatted for a few minutes more, then Benedict put down the sheaf of papers.

'This is wonderful. I can just visualise her on a rocking horse. Shall we go through a few points?'

He and Annabel went over to the desk.

'Take those rascals into the garden if you like,' the old lady suggested to Chloe. 'They like a wild dash around.'

After a few energetic games, Chloe stretched out on a swing seat. The two little dogs bounced up beside her and jostled each other for the best position in her arms.

When Benedict came out, the three of them were almost asleep.

'Are you ready to leave now or shall I pick you up later?' he asked with a laugh.

Chloe jumped guiltily and opened her eyes.

She swung her feet to the ground and Bubble and Squeak jumped down too, ready for more fun.

After goodbyes and promises to come again soon, she and Benedict set off from the village towards more open countryside.

'I liked Annabel,' she said, 'but she was a great surprise. I was expecting someone . . . ' She hesitated.

'Someone younger?'

'Well, yes.'

'Annabel might be elderly but her writing is youthful. And she's as bright as a button. She gets right inside Milly Moppet's head — remembers just what it's like to be a child.'

'How long have the two of you been working together?'

'About four years. We met at a dinner party, got talking, and found our ideas about children's books were similar. So we decided to collaborate.'

Chloe looked out of the car window

with interest as they left the houses behind.

'What magnificent views,' she said. 'Fields and woods; you can see for miles.'

'Yes, we're really quite high up here. Now, if you look ahead you can see Broadway Tower, one of the highest points of the Cotswolds.'

'Oh! Doesn't it look dramatic in the middle of open countryside? It's like Rapunzel's tower. You can just imagine her leaning over the battlements to let down her hair to her lover so that he could climb up it. Must have been very uncomfortable.'

Benedict laughed. 'You mustn't think of that. It was very romantic.'

He turned off the road on to the drive that led up to the tower.

'Oh, are we going to look at it?' Chloe asked.

'Mm. But only from the outside. Time is getting on. We'll see the inside another time. I just want to do a few sketches.'

'Sketches for your fairy book?'

'That's right. This will be your castle, Fairy Queen!'

He parked the car and they climbed out. Then he paced about until he'd found a suitable spot to sketch from and opened a camp stool. He arranged his sketching block and pencils and smiled at Chloe.

'Wander round and explore, if you like. I won't be long.'

Chloe walked slowly all round the tower. The views on all sides were incredible. She wondered how many miles she could see. As she came round to the front again, she saw Benedict waving.

'Isn't it blowy,' she said, as she came up to him. 'I nearly lost my hat.'

He was packing away his stool and sketching equipment.

'Bracing, I think the word is.'

They were glad to return to the warm car.

'I'd hoped we might be able to stop off somewhere to eat,' said Benedict,

153

'but we'd better get back. Olivia won't be pleased if we miss lunch without telling Mrs Foster. But perhaps we can have lunch out together another time?'

She wondered what they would talk about if they went out for a meal together. Benedict was very attractive, but she was still pining for Adam Raven and had no intention of allowing anything other than a strictly platonic relationship to develop between herself and her employer's son.

Back at Hampdens, she hurried to check that Mrs Keeling didn't need her.

'You have lovely pink cheeks,' the old lady said admiringly. 'The fresh air has done you good.'

She just had time to change and wash her hands before the gong sounded for lunch.

Over the meal, she told the others about where she'd been with Benedict.

'Broadway Tower. It's one of my favourite places around here,' said Olivia. 'Did you climb right to the top? There are seventy steps, I believe.'

Chloe explained that she'd only seen the outside.

'William Morris, the Victorian designer, lived there for a while,' said Mrs Keeling, 'and his artist friends like Burne-Jones and Rosetti visited. There's still a room devoted to their work.'

'I feel I'm in good artistic company when I sketch there,' Benedict put in, 'even if they are only ghosts.'

★   ★   ★

After dinner, Chloe and Mrs Keeling played draughts. Chloe had thought it might be kind to let Mrs Keeling win but soon found out that she was no match for the older lady, and had to concentrate hard not to be soundly beaten by her. They both enjoyed the game and Mrs Keeling went to bed in high spirits.

Benedict had disappeared to his studio immediately after dinner and had not reappeared, and Olivia had gone out for the evening with an old friend.

Chloe was therefore alone and feeling rather lonely. She missed Betty and their evenings together. But she wouldn't allow herself to dwell on whether or not she had done the right thing by moving away from Alderton.

She switched on the wireless. A play had started but she couldn't get into the story so she switched off the set and picked up a magazine. It fell open at an article entitled *'How To End A Relationship And Remain Friends'*, and she threw the magazine down in annoyance.

What was Adam doing now? Did he think of her? Did he care what happened to her? Was he at this moment out with Susannah Blaine? How could she stop thinking about him?

Irritably she made her way to the kitchen. Perhaps Mrs Foster would invite her to have a cup of tea and a chat. She knocked, and when there was no reply, she pushed open the door.

But the room was empty. Mrs Foster

was either in her own room, or had gone out.

Chloe made herself a cup of tea, found some biscuits and was on her way upstairs to her bedroom when the telephone in the hall began to ring.

'Hello?'

'Chloe? Is that you?'

'Betty!' Chloe's face broke into a delighted smile. 'Betty, it's so good to hear you.'

'Is anything wrong? You sound almost — well — desperate.'

'Desperate? Don't be silly. I'm just pleased to hear a familiar voice. Especially yours. Tell me all the news.'

Betty relayed all the snippets of gossip that she knew would interest her friend, never once mentioning Susannah Blaine.

'And how's my replacement?'

'Mary-Lou? She's American and a know-all. But she's good at her job. We get on all right. Aunt Ellen sends her love. She misses you and keeps hoping you'll come back.'

'D'you think I will?'

'I don't know.' Betty's voice was doubtful. 'What do you think? Do you really like it there?'

'Very much — the people, the house, the countryside. But I miss everyone at the surgery, especially you.' Her voice shook. 'And especially Adam.'

There was a pause, then Betty said, 'He keeps asking me where you've gone.'

'You haven't told him?'

'No. I said I was sworn to secrecy.'

'We had such a row when I told him what I was going to do. I didn't think he'd want to see me again.'

'Well, he does. Couldn't you — couldn't you telephone him? Just to ask how he is? Just to let him know that you're all right?'

Chloe said nothing.

'He can't telephone you,' Betty pointed out, 'if he doesn't know where you are.'

'I . . . I don't know. I'll have to think about it.'

'A call can do no harm. Put his mind at rest.'

'Oh, Betty, have I done a truly stupid thing? I love him so much. No matter what I do, I can't stop thinking about him.'

'Ring him.' Betty's voice was positive. 'I know I've said all along that you'd be best having nothing to do with him, but now I think he genuinely is missing you, and that he's worried sick about you. You're allowed to use the telephone there, aren't you? Well, ring him now. I'm going. I'll be in touch. 'Bye.'

She was gone.

Chloe replaced the receiver and sat looking into space. Should she do as Betty advised and telephone Adam? Would it stir up her doubts, or help to resolve them?

Suddenly she snatched up the receiver again, and as soon as the operator answered, gave a number. It rang a few times before a male voice answered.

Chloe swallowed and took a deep breath.

'Hello, Adam,' she said.

# Interesting News

'Cheer up, it may never happen.' Rosalyn dropped heavily on to the bench where Chloe sat gazing, unseeing, at the fountain.

'That's what I'm afraid of.' Chloe gave the gardener a wan smile.

'Anything I can help with?'

'Not unless you can think of a way for me to get to Evesham on Saturday.'

'Well, that's easily sorted. I'll take you.'

Chloe looked at the other girl in surprise. 'You'll . . . do you have a car?'

'Better than that. But why d'you want to go?' Instantly she looked apologetic. 'Sorry, I'm being nosy.'

Chloe looked down at her fingers which were pinching her skirt into little pleats. 'I . . . I wanted to meet an old friend, just for an hour or so.'

'A boyfriend?' Rosalyn leaned forward to look eagerly into her face.

'Not really. Well, sort of. He wants to see me and I don't want him to come here. I thought we could meet in Evesham; you know, a sort of halfway mark.'

'But you don't have any means of transport to get there?'

'I know there are buses, but it would take too long. I just didn't think of the problems before I agreed to go.'

Rosalyn got to her feet. 'What time do you want to set off?'

'Do you mean it? You are kind, Rosalyn. I've already asked if I can have Saturday afternoon off, so about half-past two would be fine.'

'Right you are. Be outside the garage at half-past two, then. I must go now.'

Chloe watched the gardener disappear behind a tall hedge beyond the rose garden. Probably going to get the vegetables for tonight, she thought. But what did she mean by 'better than that?' What was better than a car? Well, it really didn't matter so long as she got to Evesham.

At five to three on that Saturday afternoon, Chloe rode into the station yard at Evesham in the sidecar of Rosalyn's motorcycle.

She was stiff and a little shaken about, but after her initial embarrassment at her mode of transport, she had enjoyed the ride.

She climbed out, waved goodbye to Rosalyn who was off to see an aunt in the town, and looked around. She hoped Adam hadn't already arrived. She didn't want him to have seen her rather undignified clamber out of the sidecar.

But Adam was walking towards her, the expression on his face a mixture of incredulity and annoyance.

'Your gentleman friend didn't stay long,' he remarked.

'My gentleman friend . . . ? That was

Rosalyn, the gardener at the house where I work!'

'Rosalyn?' He looked as if he almost didn't believe her. 'A female gardener who rides a motorcycle? Where on earth have you ended up?'

'I don't think you have any right to talk like that. If it hadn't been for Rosalyn, I probably wouldn't be here.'

'I'm sorry. Forgive me. I'm so pleased you are here. How long can you stay?'

'I'm being picked up at five, so we have two hours.'

He looked her up and down. 'I'm glad you didn't have to wear motorcycle clothes. You look very pretty.'

He tucked her hand under his arm.

'Come on. Let's go and find a teashop.'

It didn't take them long to find a nice place for tea and cakes, and sitting opposite him, Chloe felt they might be back in the Viennese patisserie.

Adam gazed at her and held out his hands, palms upwards. She put her own hands into his and he grasped them tightly.

'I've missed you so much.' His voice was low so that only she could hear. 'When you left it was as if part of my life was missing.'

Chloe couldn't trust herself to speak. She almost wished she hadn't come. What if he tried to persuade her to go back? If he continued to talk like this, he might succeed.

What was she thinking of — she couldn't let down dear Mrs Keeling and she couldn't let herself down by allowing Adam to raise her hopes of a future with him when he'd already made it clear that he had no intention of making any sort of long-term commitment to her.

Oh, why had she agreed to this meeting and revived all the old doubts again?

Adam released her hands and picked up the menu.

'Tea and cakes, or would you prefer something more substantial?'

'Tea and cakes will be lovely.'

He gave her his warmest smile. And how his face lit up when he smiled, she thought.

'I'm sorry, but I can't help saying it — I'm so pleased to see you again.'

The waitress appeared and Adam gave their order.

While they waited for their food, he told her all about the new nurse and how she bullied all the doctors and got away with it.

'The American one?'

'Yes. She's American and very tough.' He laughed. 'I think even Dr Blaine is afraid of her.'

Chloe joined in the laughter.

Their tea arrived and Chloe picked up the teapot.

Adam studied the cakes.

'Not very creamy. Certainly not Viennese.'

He took a custard tart.

'But probably better for you.' Chloe passed him a cup of tea. 'Do you still go to the patisserie on Saturdays after the library?'

'Without you?' He looked reproachful.

'Tell me what else has happened at the surgery,' she said, to lighten the atmosphere.

'Well, something very nice happened yesterday. Mrs Shelley had her twins, one of each, and says she will call the boy Adam, after me.'

'How lovely. That's a compliment.'

They drank their tea and sat lost in their individual thoughts.

Then Adam, with a sigh, said, 'We have to talk about it, don't we?'

'Talk about . . . ?'

'You know what I mean. Your sudden departure. How we feel. Are you happy?'

'I'm not going to think about being happy. I just want to forget about you, Adam.'

'But I'll never forget you, Chloe. I'll be waiting until you come to your senses and come back. Then we can start again.'

'Come to my senses? You're the one

who wanted no commitment. I know exactly what I'm doing.'

'Do you know what you're doing to me?'

'I'm sure life has its compensations for you.'

'So we're back to Susannah?'

'Don't let's talk about Susannah.'

'But she was the problem, wasn't she?'

'I won't talk about her. Let's change the subject.'

'Very well. Where are you living now? Betty wouldn't tell me anything.'

'I told you, I swore her to secrecy.'

'But, Chloe, I've been thinking about us.'

He spoke urgently as if aware that time was going by and nothing had been resolved.

'What if we had a secret engagement — secret for about a year? No-one would know, so it wouldn't affect my relationship with Dr Blaine, but we'd know, and you'd feel more secure.'

She looked at him without speaking

for a few moments, then she said flatly, 'A secret engagement.'

He said nothing, as if suddenly wary of the tone of her voice.

'A secret engagement,' she repeated. 'No announcement, no ring, no-one to know that someone cares enough for me to want to marry me.'

'Oh, Chloe,' he pleaded, 'you know why.'

She stood up and picked up her bag.

'No, thank you, Adam. If you can't acknowledge me as your fiancée, then we'll remain just friends.'

She glanced at her watch.

'Now, will you walk me back to the station, please? Rosalyn will be there to collect me in ten minutes.'

They walked along in silence. As they reached the station, Adam stopped and took her arm.

'We'll do this again, won't we? I must know how you're getting on.'

She gave him a faint smile. 'Let's leave it for a little while. But I might get back in touch.'

'Can you forgive me?' His expression was tragic.

'Forgive you for what? You thought your suggestion a solution, I didn't. There's nothing to forgive.'

He took her hands.

'Goodbye, Chloe. Thank you for coming. I'll be waiting to hear from you.'

She left him and walked quickly across to where Rosalyn was standing by her motorcycle. She climbed into the sidecar and looked straight ahead through tear-filled eyes.

With one glance at Adam, Rosalyn swung herself into the saddle, kicked the starter and with a roar, they were out of the station yard and on to the road back to Hampdens.

It was a beautiful autumn. The garden was beginning to glow with orange and brown and gold tints. There were many trees and the lawns were covered with red and copper leaves.

Benedict came into the room as Chloe and Mrs Keeling were admiring the view beyond the garden window.

'How do you feel about being a fairy queen today?' he asked Chloe.

She had hoped he was joking when he'd mentioned it before. Obviously he hadn't been.

'I've sorted out some clothes,' Mrs Keeling said, giving her son a conspiratorial smile. 'We'll go upstairs and Chloe can try them on.'

She swept Chloe before her up the stairs and into her bedroom.

Ten minutes later, Chloe was dressed in a long brocade dress which, from its old-fashioned style, must have been worn by Mrs Keeling in her youth.

The old lady pinned floating voile panels from each of Chloe's shoulders.

'They're curtain panels,' she said, 'but no-one will know.'

She then produced a long silver wig from heaven knew where, and set a beautiful diamanté tiara on the girl's head before propelling her towards a mirrored door.

Chloe looked at her reflection and blushed.

She liked dressing for an evening out, but this was unreal, theatrical.

Mrs Keeling fluttered around in the background, adjusting Chloe's wig and draperies.

She was enjoying herself.

'This reminds me of when I was young,' she twittered. 'We were always going to fancy dress parties. Dressing up was very popular. I think it's such a shame young people don't enjoy it so much nowadays. There, I think you'll do. Let's go and show Benedict.'

Chloe went downstairs feeling very self-conscious. Benedict studied her, but without any interest in her as a person. He was looking at her as a prospective fairy queen.

'You're perfect,' he said. 'Now come on and we'll get started.'

They paraded through the garden, Benedict carrying a chair for his mother who was still chattering, and Chloe holding up her long skirt and praying that they wouldn't bump into Rosalyn.

She was sure the gardener would be unable to keep her face straight when she saw Chloe's costume.

To her relief, they reached Benedict's prepared corner unseen. He had set up his stool and easel facing a grassy bank and he motioned Chloe to sit down there.

'Try to forget that you're posing,' he instructed. 'Just sit naturally.' He sketched furiously with long flowing movements. 'Now can you stand by that tree? Put your hands on the trunk. Lovely. Now look back over your shoulder. Now look at me.'

Chloe began to lose her self-consciousness in the interest of what they were doing. Mrs Keeling watched closely, but said nothing. She had been warned in advance, by her son, not to interfere.

After an hour, Mrs Foster appeared with a tray and they all took a break and sat and enjoyed the coffee and biscuits.

It was a beautiful morning and Chloe thought of her friends back at the surgery, kept indoors by their work, while she was free to enjoy the lovely autumn days in the garden.

Benedict took a camera from its case. 'Can we just go through the poses again while I take some pictures to work from when I'm back in the studio?'

Chloe had no trouble remembering what she had done the first time, and Benedict nodded approvingly as he clicked away. At last he replaced his camera, packed away his pencils, and put his easel under his arm.

'Come along, you two, it'll be lunch-time soon.'

Chloe and Mrs Keeling began to walk together towards the house, Chloe feeling a tiny twinge of annoyance with Benedict. She'd done everything he'd asked, dressed up, posed as he wanted, and he hadn't even thanked her.

She knew she was just his model, but surely even models should be thanked, and a tiny voice inside her told her that he could have said how nice she looked.

When they reached the house, Mrs Keeling went inside and Benedict turned away to go to his studio. Then he stopped and came back to Chloe.

'Thank you, Chloe. You looked so beautiful, I know these illustrations will be a success.'

And he bent and kissed her forehead.

Chloe watched him walk away, colour flooding her cheeks. So he *had* noticed. She floated into the house and up the stairs to her room like the fairy queen she was supposed to be.

In the bedroom, she studied her

reflection in the full-length-mirror. Why did she care whether Benedict Keeling admired her? Just female pride, she supposed. Her self confidence was fragile after her meeting with Adam; to be ignored by any man was too much to bear.

*   *   *

The autumn days continued mild and sunny and Chloe woke each morning with a keen anticipation of what the day might bring.

Her duties were light. Mrs Keeling was woken each morning by the housekeeper with a cup of tea and when she had drunk it, she rang a bell for Chloe, who drew a bath and helped Mrs Keeling to bathe and dress. Then they breakfasted together in the sunny dining-room overlooking the kitchen garden and they often watched Rosalyn there, busying herself with the fruit and vegetables they enjoyed each day.

Sometimes Mrs Keeling was wistful.

'I do miss my gardening. I used to help in the kitchen garden, you know,' she said proudly. 'I didn't just weed and grow flowers.'

'I have an idea. Perhaps Rosalyn could make you a raised bed,' suggested Chloe. 'Then you could sit on a chair and garden. You could only grow flowers, I suppose, but it would be better than nothing.'

'What a good idea. Let's speak to Rosalyn about it.'

Mrs Keeling was instantly enthusiastic and, tapping on the window, beckoned Rosalyn to come and see her.

Puzzled, the gardener made her way to the kitchen where she could change her boots for shoes and wash her hands. Then she came through to the dining-room where she accepted a cup of coffee from Chloe.

'We've had an idea,' said Mrs Keeling, giving Chloe a quick look to see if she was going to challenge the 'we'.

She explained the idea to Rosalyn

and for the next half-hour, the two of them discussed a possible position for the raised bed and thought about what could be grown in it.

'It's a bit late in the year,' Rosalyn cautioned. 'We could do it for next spring.'

'No. We'll do it now. I can prepare the soil and, through the winter, I can decide what I'd like to grow.'

Rosalyn caught Chloe's eye. Chloe gave her a little smile. She had already discovered that Mrs Keeling's enthusiasms were quickly roused and that once they were, she would never take no for an answer.

Rosalyn went back to her work having agreed to make a start on the raised bed during the next few days.

Mrs Keeling turned to Chloe with a satisfied smile. 'That was a good idea! I can't wait to get started.' She seemed to be filled with a surge of energy. 'Shall we go out somewhere for our morning coffee today?' she suggested. 'Maybe we can take a little drive around first.'

'I should like that,' said Chloe. 'Where would you like to go?'

'Let me think. What about Broadway? Do you know it?'

'I came through there on my first day. It was very busy!'

'That was a weekend and earlier in the year. It won't be too crowded today.'

In no time, a car from the local garage was waiting at the door.

'This is Sam,' Mrs Keeling introduced the driver to Chloe. 'He drives me around when I don't want to bother Benedict.'

Chloe smiled to herself as she settled her employer in the back seat with a rug over her knees. She had been secretly imagining exploring the area on the back of Rosalyn's motorcycle, with Mrs Keeling tucked into the sidecar!

Mrs Keeling conferred with Sam and they were soon driving down narrow lanes and through tiny, sleepy villages with houses all built of the same soft golden stone.

'We've come a rather round-about route,' confessed the old lady, 'but I wanted to show you some places that you won't have seen yet. Here we are, the main street of Broadway.'

It was a lovely sunny morning, so Sam parked the car in the cool shade of a spreading tree.

Chloe, with Mrs Keeling leaning on her arm, strolled slowly down the street which she had studied so eagerly a few weeks before. Now she could look into the interesting shop windows and admire the little houses.

'This is my favourite teashop,' said Mrs Keeling, stopping outside a window which displayed a tempting range of cakes and chocolates.

Inside, Chloe was surprised to find herself in a long, narrow room, bright with pictures and gifts for sale. Down the centre were round tables, prettily laid with flowered tablecloths that hung to the floor. The waitresses in ankle-length skirts and aprons seemed to have stepped from an earlier age.

'Shall we have coffee and scones?' Mrs Keeling settled herself at a table. 'They're nice and buttery here.'

'You're not supposed to have too much butter,' scolded Chloe.

'But this is a special occasion,' her employer wheedled. 'Our first trip out together.'

Chloe relented. 'Well, just this once. But I won't allow it next time. I'm supposed to be looking after you, remember.'

Mrs Keeling patted her hand. 'You look after me very well.'

The waitress appeared. They gave their order and settled back in their seats. Mrs Keeling eyed Chloe speculatively.

'Do you like Benedict?'

Chloe was startled. Would she tell his mother if she didn't like him? She considered.

'He has a charm all his own.'

'I know what you mean. But he won't put himself out to get a girlfriend.'

'To get a girlfriend? Is that what he wants?'

'He must. Everyone wants someone of their own. Someone to love and take an interest in them. A companion.'

Their order arrived and there was silence for a while as they ate their scones, which certainly were buttery.

Chloe considered Mrs Keeling's remarks.

'I think perhaps *you* want him to find someone,' she suggested at last. '*I* think he's too wrapped up in his work.'

'That's all very well. His work is important to him, of course. He's successful and wants to do even better. But, yes, I would like him to find someone. I hate to think of him always alone.'

'But he has friends.'

'It's not the same. I blame Magda.' Mrs Keeling took another scone and wiped her fingers. 'See — I told you — buttery.'

Chloe smiled at her. 'Well, enjoy them. I won't let you have any more for a long time. Er — who is Magda?'

Mrs Keeling sipped her coffee,

replaced her cup and wiped her lips before speaking.

'Magda was a visitor to the village six years ago. She came from France to improve her English. She was beautiful, I suppose, with black hair and olive skin, but she was hard. Hard and calculating. Benedict fell madly in love with her.'

'And she with him?' Chloe queried.

'Oh, no. Oh, she pretended to be interested. He took her all over the place, which suited her very well. But when she suddenly decided to return to France, nothing he could say would keep her here. I don't know for sure, but I expect he offered her marriage.'

'Would you like him to have married her?'

'No! I didn't like the girl. But I would like him to have forgotten her quickly and found someone else.'

'You think he hasn't got over her?'

'I'm sure he hasn't. He never talks about her but I just have a feeling.' She gave Chloe a sideways look. 'That's why

I wondered whether you liked him. I'm sure he is interested in you.'

Chloe was alarmed. 'Oh, no. I'm sure he isn't. Please, Mrs Keeling, don't think along those lines. It's impossible.'

'Impossible? You have someone already?'

Then she saw the look of distress on Chloe's face and said hastily, 'I'm sorry, my dear. That was wrong of me. I mustn't pry.'

Chloe poured more coffee for them both as she tried to calm her emotions.

To cover the awkward moment, Mrs Keeling looked around the café. 'They have some very pretty gifts here, trays, pictures, ornaments. Just the place if you should ever need to purchase a present for someone.'

Chloe, now recovered, followed her gaze.

'I might buy a tray with a Cotswold picture on it for my friend Betty,' she said.

'Your best friend?'

'Yes, I suppose she is. We worked together at the surgery in Alderton and

I lived with her and her aunt.'

'Do you miss her? You haven't had a chance to make many friends here.'

'I do miss her,' Chloe admitted, 'but we telephone each other and write often. Perhaps I shall go back and see her one weekend soon.'

'I have an idea,' said Mrs Keeling. 'Why don't you invite her to stay? She could come for a week, if you like.'

'That would be lovely! Thank you! We'd both enjoy that. I'll mention it next time I speak to her.'

Glad to have brought a smile back to the face of her young companion, Mrs Keeling stood up and collected her gloves and bag.

'Let's have a little walk around the village before we return.'

On the way out, Chloe chose a small tray with a chocolate box picture of a pretty Cotswold cottage in a flowery garden, and Mrs Keeling bought a pot of local honey.

'Come along, my dear.' Mrs Keeling took her arm. 'We'll walk down to the bottom of the street and back up, then we'll go home for lunch.'

* ⋆ ⋆ ⋆

Benedict joined them for lunch but seemed preoccupied. When he had finished eating, he turned to Chloe.

'I've finished some of the fairy sketches. Would you like to see them?'

'I can't leave Mrs Keeling,' she said apologetically. 'Can I come this evening?'

'I shall be out this evening.' He stood up. 'Perhaps some other time.'

'Chloe can come up to the studio at half-past two,' said his mother. 'I shall have a rest then. I'm quite tired after my walk this morning.'

Benedict made them a little bow.

'Very well,' he said. 'Half-past two it is then.'

Chloe made her employer comfortable on her day-bed at twenty-past two, but the old lady decided she might not sleep, and sent Chloe to her bedroom for a book.

The clock was chiming the half-hour when Chloe at last hurried from the drawing-room.

As she climbed the spiral staircase, she worried that Benedict might have thought she'd changed my mind, but he seemed not to have noticed the time and barely looked up as she entered the studio.

'I may change some of them later,' he said, as he handed her a sheaf of stiff papers, 'but I'm quite pleased with these.'

Chloe gasped as she studied the first drawing.

The fairy queen was reclined on a grassy bank with a group of shadowy elves and fairies around her, and although the fairy looked like her, the features were pointed and elongated in true fairy fashion.

'They're lovely illustrations,' she said, looking at first one then another, with a feeling of pride.

'You were a good model. I wanted

the effect of your hair and your draperies flowing behind you as you walked and I think I've captured that.'

'Has Annabel written the stories?'

'No. A French writer. These are for my French publisher.'

A thought struck Chloe. 'Do you often need to go to France — to see your publisher, I mean.'

'Quite often. But I don't really need an excuse. I just love to go there.'

Magda went home to France, thought Chloe. Does he visit Magda? Is that why he won't find a girlfriend? But why keep it a secret?

Benedict held out a hand for the sketches.

'I'll show you some more when they're finished.'

Chloe glanced at her watch.

'I'd better go. Thank you for letting me see them. I'm most impressed.' She smiled at him but he'd already turned away and picked up a charcoal stick.

Chloe left the studio without another word.

★   ★   ★

Betty telephoned her that evening agog with news.

'I have some news for you, too,' said Chloe. 'But tell me yours first.'

'No. You first.'

'Very well. Mrs Keeling says I may invite you to stay for a week. Would you come?'

'I'd love to see all the people and places you talk about. When can I come?'

'We're going to London for a day or two soon. When we get back, I'll write to you. I'll tell her you love the idea. Now then, what's your news?'

'It's about Adam — Adam and Susannah.'

'Oh, yes?' Chloe's voice was wary.

'There's been a dreadful row! It was after surgery hours, when we were all getting ready to go home. Susannah arrived to go out to dinner with her father and spotted Adam in the corridor. She was being her usual silly self and began to tease him and ask him when he was going to take her dancing.'

'And what did Adam say?'

'She was only teasing him, but he's been in a very difficult mood lately; ever since he went to visit you in Evesham, in fact. You can't ask him anything without getting a snappy answer.'

'What did he say?'

'He told her to stop chasing him. He said that he had no intention of taking her anywhere and that she was to leave him alone. I could hear it all because I'd just opened the door of our room ready to go home.'

'So what happened then?' Chloe felt a perverse thrill to think that Susannah wasn't getting her own way, though underneath she felt sorry for the younger girl.

'Susannah burst into tears and at that moment Dr Blaine came round the corner.'

'Oh my goodness. Poor Adam!'

'It was poor Susannah, really. She hadn't meant any harm. Dr Blaine hurried her out and said that he'd speak to Adam in the morning. What do you think of that?'

'Well, I wonder what will happen tomorrow?'

'I'll let you know. Did anything happen when you met Adam — anything that could have made him so bad-tempered?'

'It wasn't a happy meeting. I wondered whether the whole idea hadn't been a mistake.'

'He loves you, Chloe. I realise that now.'

'I think I know that. And I love him. But I need to be sure.'

'You can't think he has any feelings for Susannah after what I've told you tonight.'

'No. But I've never thought he did have feelings for her. That was part of the problem.'

# An Exciting Day Out

As they glided through the country lanes, heading for London in Benedict's big, comfortable car, Chloe contrasted the journey with her trip to London with Betty.

Then, she had been nervous and anxious, wondering about the interview ahead and whether she wanted such a momentous change in her life.

Now, settled in her new job with new people who were rapidly becoming her friends, she could relax and enjoy the trip.

She sat in the front of the car with Benedict while Mrs Keeling, covered with a rug and surrounded by pillows, travelled in state in the back.

'When shall we stop for coffee? I'd like to stretch my legs,' the old lady called to Benedict.

'Really, Mama, we've only been going

for twenty minutes. We'll stop, but not yet. Why don't you have a little sleep?'

'Good idea. As soon as we reach a boring main road, I shall.'

Five minutes later, Chloe, peeping over her shoulder, saw that her employer hadn't waited for the boring main road but was already fast asleep.

'Good,' said Benedict when she told him. 'Now we can get a move on in peace.'

The motion of the car was so smooth that Chloe thought she might have difficulty staying awake herself.

'Do you often go to London?' asked Benedict.

'Very seldom, though I trained there. I'm happier in the country. I don't like rush and bustle. But, of course,' she added hastily, 'the occasional trip is very interesting.'

'You're staying at Olivia's hotel,' he informed her.

'Yes, I know. But aren't you?'

'No. I have people to see — my publisher for one. And I may pop across to Paris tomorrow.'

He said this so casually that Chloe glanced across at him to see if he was joking. To her, a trip to France would be a holiday, not a one-day visit.

'To see your French publisher?'

'Er — yes. That's it. We join the main road just ahead. Then we can really cover some miles. Are you comfortable?'

This seemed an attempt to change the subject, so she assured him that she was and looked out of the window. The season was wearing on now and the trees were gradually being denuded of their leaves and the fields had a stubbly, uncared-for appearance.

Mrs Keeling awoke just as Benedict was turning into a large country house hotel car park.

'This looks very pleasant,' he said. 'We'll get coffee here.'

Coffee and biscuits were served in a dark, comfortable lounge. Mrs Keeling and Benedict took their surroundings for granted, but Chloe looked around with interest.

There were large, squashy sofas and huge oil paintings of country scenes in heavy gilt frames. The only sound was the deep tick of a grandfather clock in the corner.

But they were soon on their way again and, after a mile or two, joined the busy main road to London. The big car purred along.

Chloe looked at Benedict's long, slim, artist's fingers on the steering wheel.

'I should have thought you'd like a sports car,' she said.

'Why?' He gave her an astonished glanced. 'Do you think I am a road hog? Am I going too fast for you?'

'No. I'm sorry. Was that an insult?'

'Not at all. I did have one once, actually. It was fun for a few years but the novelty wore off.'

Looking back later, it seemed to Chloe that they had chatted idly all the way to London, yet at the end of the journey she felt she knew no more about him than when they started out. Any question bordering — however slightly — on the personal, was fielded by Benedict and the subject changed. He seemed to have a wall around him which no-one was to breach.

By the time they reached London, Chloe was looking forward to getting out and stretching her legs. She was hungry, too, but no-one had mentioned lunch.

As if in answer to her thoughts, Mrs Keeling said, 'We'll be there in twenty minutes. Olivia will have sandwiches and drinks waiting for us. I'm sure you young things feel peckish.'

They pulled up outside the Avon Court Hotel at almost exactly the time that Benedict had promised when they'd set off, and Olivia was waiting for them on the steps.

Benedict disappeared with the car to park it behind the hotel while his sister took her mother and Chloe to her little sitting-room where, sure enough, sandwiches and tiny cakes with coffee and wine awaited them on a table in the window.

Chloe found it strange to be back in this room again. Mother and daughter had so much to say to each other, that she was able to gaze from the window at the busy street and marvel at the constant stream of traffic and the people scurrying in all directions like ants.

Suddenly she became aware that Olivia was speaking to her.

'I asked whether there is anything you would like to do while you're in London.'

'Well . . . I shall look after Mrs Keeling as usual.' Chloe wasn't quite sure what to say.

'Mother will rest all this afternoon,' Olivia decided. 'If she is to see her specialist tomorrow, she must be calm and relaxed. I shall tuck her up in bed for a few hours and you may go out if you like.'

Chloe sat and thought. She had rushed around London with Betty but she wasn't sure how she would enjoy it on her own. Then an idea struck her.

'What I would really like,' she began, 'is a tour on an open-topped bus. I wanted to do that when I was here for my interview,' she told them shyly, 'but there wasn't time.'

'We have all the information on the open-topped bus tours at the desk in the foyer,' said Olivia. 'When you're ready, I'll telephone down and get someone to help you.'

⋆   ⋆   ⋆

When Chloe rejoined Mrs Keeling and Olivia for tea in the hotel diningroom several hours later, she was bubbling with enthusiasm.

'It was wonderful, and I think I've seen the whole of London — Buckingham Palace, the Tower, St Paul's, Westminster Abbey. Every time I thought we were coming to the end of the tour, we turned into another road and there were still more sights to be seen.'

'And, of course, you saw the River Thames?' asked Olivia.

'Oh, I didn't just see it! I went on the river. Just a little way, but it was fun. Then we climbed back on to the bus and off we went again.'

Olivia passed her a cup of tea. 'You must be ready for this.'

'I am, and I'm afraid I'm dreadfully hungry.'

'Perhaps these sandwiches are rather small for a hungry person.' Mrs Keeling smiled at her. 'But eat up, we can order more.'

Olivia, who had a flat not far from the hotel, appeared the next morning just as Mrs Keeling and Chloe were finishing their breakfast.

'Any sign of Benedict?' she asked, accepting a cup of coffee from Chloe.

'No. He's disappeared somewhere. I didn't ask where he was going,' said his mother airily. 'He'll turn up.'

Chloe thought of his remark about popping over to Paris but didn't mention it. Perhaps he wouldn't want his mother and sister to know what he was up to.

'I've ordered a taxi for half-past nine,' said Olivia, looking up at the ornate clock on the wall. 'We have nearly half an hour before we set off for the doctor's surgery, Mother.' Then, 'What do you plan to do this afternoon?' she asked Chloe.

'Well — this isn't supposed to be a holiday for me,' protested the girl. 'Isn't there anything useful I can do?'

'Take breaks where you can,' advised Mrs Keeling. 'We won't be back in London for another six months so make the most of it.'

'And I'm taking Mother to visit Aunt Imogen this afternoon,' said Olivia. 'You would be bored to tears, so you must think of something interesting to do while we're out.'

'I saw the sights yesterday so I might do some shopping today.'

'Good idea,' said Mrs Keeling. 'Just what I'd do if I could. But big shops are so tiring.'

Ten minutes later, while they were in Mrs Keeling's room collecting her coat, the old lady pressed a little roll of money into Chloe's hand and before the girl could refuse, she said, 'I meant what I told you; I should love to go shopping but I can't. So you enjoy it for me. Buy yourself a pretty dress. No more objections. Come on! Olivia, will be waiting.'

The heart specialist's rooms in Harley Street bore little resemblance to the surgery where Chloe had worked. Mr Symons' quarters were sumptuously decorated and furnished and a glamorous receptionist got up from behind her antique desk in the hall to conduct Mrs Keeling and her entourage to a comfortable lounge.

'Mr Symons will see you in five minutes,' she murmured and went out, softly closing the door behind her.

In less than five minutes, a door in the far wall opened and a small, plump, highly-polished man came into the room. He glowed with cleanliness and his bald head shone like his perfectly manicured fingernails.

'Dear Mrs Keeling.' He took her hand. 'And Miss Keeling. And whom have we here?'

'This is Miss Perle, my marvellous nurse-companion.'

Chloe's fingers were lightly pressed.

'Would you wait here while I speak to Mrs and Miss Keeling? I'll have a word with you afterwards. Help yourself to coffee.'

He gestured towards a table in the corner.

Chloe poured herself a cup from the silver pot, chose a magazine from a table nearby, and settled herself to wait.

She was just finishing her drink when the door to the consulting room opened and the doctor called her into the surgery.

'Well, Miss Perle. I'm pleased to say that Mrs Keeling is very much better than when I examined her six months ago. She says it is mainly due to you. You've brought some new interests into her life.'

Chloe coloured. She hadn't expected praise like this.

'I'm . . . I'm so glad Mrs Keeling is doing well,' she stammered.

'Continue with whatever you've been doing.'

He beamed at her and then turned back to his patient.

'Lots of rest, but increase the gentle

exercise. You can't do better than a short walk or two each day. I shall see you again in another six months.'

*  *  *

The taxi taking Mrs Keeling and Olivia on their visit to their Aunt Imogen dropped off Chloe in Oxford Street.

She had studied her map and knew that when she tired of the shops there she could move on to Regent Street without having to walk too far. She'd promised to be back at the hotel by five, which gave her plenty of time for shopping.

She paused for a moment, amazed at the amount of traffic on the London streets. Buses, lorries, cars of all sorts — even an open carriage — all flowed along in a continuous stream. She dreaded the time when she might need to cross the road.

On her previous visit with Betty, Chloe had been propelled in and out of shops by her friend without a chance to look at the beautifully decorated windows. Now, on her own, she could stroll slowly, gazing at the window displays and marvelling at the variety of goods on offer.

There was little she really needed, apart from some new walking shoes and a warm jacket, so she decided to concentrate first on choosing a dress to buy with the money her employer had given her. It would be rude to return with nothing when Mrs Keeling had wanted her to enjoy the pleasure of shopping in the city.

She decided that an evening dress would be a waste of money. She still had, hanging in her wardrobe, the beautiful ice-blue gown she had worn to the Chateau Belmont with Adam. It brought back rather sad memories but she couldn't afford to get rid of it and it would be useful if she had an important evening engagement.

No, she would find something less formal to spend Mrs Keeling's money on.

On the ground floor of a large department store she found herself standing in front of the lifts. She usually used stairs for the sake of fitness but, as she stood there, wondering whether to go up to the model gowns in the lift for a change, the doors slid open.

The tall, handsome man who stepped out in front of her was as startled to see her as she was to see him.

'Chloe!' In two strides he had grasped both her hands and was looking into her eyes.

'Adam! Whatever are you doing in London?'

Then, embarrassed, she realised that they were being regarded with interest by the queue of shoppers waiting for the next lift.

'We can't stand here, we're in the way.'

Flustered, she drew him to one side.

'I came up on business,' he explained. 'I only have a couple of hours before my train. How long do you have?'

'About the same, but . . . '

'Then we mustn't waste time. Where can we go to talk?'

'There's a restaurant on the top floor,' she suggested.

'Come on.' He drew her towards the lifts.

'But first I must buy a dress,' she insisted. 'It's why I'm here.'

'But you can buy a dress at any time,' he protested, exasperated.

'I can't. I'm going back tomorrow.'

'Back where?'

'Home,' she said shortly. He wasn't going to catch her like that. 'It won't take long. I know what I want.'

He sighed loudly but gave in, and they stepped off the lift on the dress floor.

Chloe began to inspect a rail of garments.

'I want something not too dressy, but suitable for evenings.' She frowned as she studied the selection. 'But not an evening dress.'

'I can't believe we're wasting time doing this,' he said, groaning.

'Help me, then, and I shall be quicker.'

'I don't know anything about dresses.' He grabbed at a hanger. 'What about this?'

'I hate brown.'

'Or this?'

'Too plain.'

'This one isn't plain.'

'Too fussy.'

'Chloe!'

'This could be it.'

She lifted out a dress in a beautiful sage green with a tiny jacket to cover the draped bodice.

'I won't be a moment,' she told him, and disappeared into the fitting-room.

When she came out wearing the dress, Adam gave a low whistle.

'Beautiful, but it looks awfully expensive.'

'That's all right. My employer gave me some money and insisted I buy a dress. That's why I had to get one now.'

She whisked back into the fitting-room.

When she came out, Adam was waiting with a glowering face.

'Just a minute. Why did he give you money to buy a dress?'

'She's not a he, she's an elderly lady. Don't waste time being jealous, Adam.'

Ten minutes later, they were sitting in the restaurant, hidden in a corner behind a curved wooden partition.

She picked up the menu. 'What shall we have?'

'I want this first . . . ' He folded her in his arms and kissed her passionately.

'Oh, Chloe, I miss you so much. The fates are being kind to us. Even a short time is better than nothing.'

As the waitress appeared, they moved swiftly apart and he gave their order.

'Betty told me you'd had an argument with Dr Blaine — about Susannah,' Chloe ventured.

'The girl's a pest, but I think she's got the message now.' He gazed at her. 'I hope you have too.'

She was spared an answer by the arrival of the sandwiches, tea and cakes.

'Are you happy, Chloe?'

'You asked me that the last time you saw me. But yes, I'm content, for the moment.'

'And how long will that moment be?'

'Oh, Adam, can we talk about something else? Do you want this cake? You like iced ones, don't you?'

He looked at his watch. 'One hour more together and we talk about cakes.'

'What was your business meeting about?' Chloe made a determined effort to change the subject.

'I had to go to the American Embassy.'

'The American Embassy? Oh yes, your brother works in America, doesn't he? Was it about him?'

'Not exactly.'

He seemed disinclined to talk about it and changed the subject in his turn.

'How long have you been up in London?'

They chatted for a while about mundane things, then Adam stood up.

'I'll have to be going. Can you come

to the station with me?'

'Of course. Then I'll get a taxi back to my hotel. I don't want to wander round the shops any more.'

In the taxi to the station, they sat close together, their hands entwined.

'When shall I see you again?'

'I can't say. Soon. I'll call you.'

'Chloe.' He turned to look into her eyes. 'I don't think I can go on like this. Can't you see it's not fair? We belong together. I can't just forget about you. I can't just pretend you don't mean anything to me. Don't you feel the same?'

Once again, she was plagued by doubts. Was she doing the right thing? Should she go back to Alderton and let events take their course? Should she even agree to his secret engagement idea?

But he still hadn't said he loved her. He expected everything from her but she had to take his devotion on trust.

But she couldn't change direction now. She was committed to Mrs Keeling.

She made no answer but turned away so that he couldn't see the tears which threatened to fill her eyes.

They reached the station.

'Let's say goodbye now,' she urged. 'I won't come to the train. I can't face protracted goodbyes.'

He held her tightly. 'Dearest Chloe.'

He opened the taxi door and was gone into the milling crowds.

The driver looked over his shoulder at his remaining passenger.

'Where to, Miss?'

'Avon Court Hotel, please,' she said, and sank back into her seat, squeezing her eyes tight shut to stop the tears.

★ ★ ★

After an hour in her room, Chloe was once more quite composed when she went to Mrs Keeling's room to show her the dress.

'Oh, my dear, it's lovely. I hope you'll soon have an opportunity to wear it.'

The opportunity came sooner than

they expected. When they went down to the lounge for some tea, Benedict was waiting for them.

'So, you've returned,' said his mother, as he kissed her cheek. 'Is this a flying visit or are you staying for dinner?'

'Will Olivia be here for dinner?' he asked.

'Yes.'

'Well, I did wonder — since in that case you won't be on your own — whether you'd let me take Chloe out to dine?'

'If Chloe would like to go, I think it's an excellent idea,' said his mother.

Mother and son both turned to look at Chloe, who had herself been looking forward to a quiet meal at the hotel followed by some time alone in her room to think about Adam and their meeting this afternoon.

Now she had to smile and look pleased at Benedict's suggestion.

'You could wear your new dress,' said Mrs Keeling.

So, at half-past seven that evening,

Chloe found herself sitting in Benedict's car, heading for the bright lights.

'I've been told of a new place that's really rather different.' Benedict smiled. 'It's called *The Sheikh of Araby*. I thought we'd try it.'

The restaurant certainly was different! Chloe stared in astonishment as they entered the circular dining-room which had been designed to look like the interior of a Bedouin tent. The sides and ceiling of the room were draped with red and gold material held in place by looped gold cords and tassels. The more adventurous patrons sat on deep cushions at low tables, but Chloe and Benedict followed the waiter to one of the more conventional tables near the centre of the room.

'The waiters look like Ali Baba's forty thieves,' she whispered as they studied their menus.

In the background, sensuous music played softly, and exotic perfume filled the air.

'I wouldn't be surprised if the cabaret

turns out to be a snake charmer!' he whispered back.

Chloe was relieved to see that there was English food on the menu. She didn't feel able to tackle the strange dishes being carried past their tables to other diners.

'I love your dress,' said Benedict, when they had ordered their food and were cradling glasses of a delicious wine.

'It was a present from your mother,' she said. 'I bought it today.'

I bought it today with my darling Adam, and I'm wearing it with you, she thought.

Their first course arrived, a delicate pink and green salmon and sorrel roulade.

'This is delicious,' Chloe enthused after her first taste. 'Is it really prepared by an Arabian chef?'

Benedict laughed. 'No Arabian chef, I'm afraid. In fact, I don't suppose many of the staff are anything other than Londoners. But they have a

French chef. I fancy he prepared this.'

'Did you go to France?' Chloe asked.

'Mm. Yesterday. I came back this morning.'

'You have a French publisher?'

'Yes. I'm glad to say Milly Moppet is translated into French and sells very well.'

'She looks like a little French child, doesn't she?'

'Yes,' he answered vaguely, 'I suppose she does.'

Their next course arrived — a Camembert and leek tart for Chloe and braised lamb for Benedict.

They sniffed appreciatively at the rich aromas, then picked up their cutlery.

'You were a nurse in the Midlands, weren't you, before you came to look after Mother? Is that where you were brought up?'

'Oh, no. I lived most of my childhood on the Welsh border.'

'Which is why you don't have a Midlands accent,' he commented. 'Do your parents still live there?'

'They died in a boating accident when I was three,' she said. 'I don't remember them.'

'So you were brought up by . . . ?'

'My brother and his wife. My stepbrother, actually. He's years older than me. Luckily he was prepared to take me on. We have very few other relations.'

They ate in silence for a while, enjoying the food.

Then Chloe asked, 'What sort of childhood did you have?'

'A very conventional one, actually. We've always lived at Hampdens. My father died five years ago. I went away to school then to art college, but apart from that, I've hardly left the Cotswolds.'

'Except to go to France,' she said with a laugh.

Before he could answer, two men appeared and carried a large round basket with a lid into the centre of the room.

Chloe and Benedict watched with interest.

The men were followed by an old man with a white beard who was wearing a turban and flowing robes. He carried a long musical pipe.

'I told you — a snake charmer,' said Benedict.

'Oh, no!' Chloe turned alarmed eyes towards him. 'I thought you were joking. I don't like snakes.'

He put a hand on her arm. 'Don't worry. It's a rather large basket for a snake. I think we're in for a surprise.'

The old man lifted the pipe to his lips and began to play a rippling, swaying tune. The room was silent, waiting. Then the basket lid was cast aside and two slim arms twined upwards. They were followed by the sinuous body of a young woman dressed in a tight green and gold costume.

As she stepped out of the basket and began to dance, Chloe relaxed and sat back to enjoy the performance.

When the dancer, back in her basket, had been carried from the room followed by the old man, Chloe joined in the wild applause.

'A cabaret with a difference,' Benedict commented. 'What would you like now?'

'Nothing more, thank you,' said Chloe. 'Just coffee.'

'We won't stay too long,' he said. 'I expect Mama will want to see you before she settles for the night. And we have a long journey home tomorrow.'

'This has been a lovely few days,' said Chloe, and she wasn't just thinking of the afternoon with Adam. The whole family had been so kind to her.

'Mama has a check-up every six months so there'll be more breaks like this. She said that her doctor was very pleased with the way you've looked after her.'

'I've become very fond of her and she's a delight to care for.'

⋆　⋆　⋆

Benedict dropped her off at the bottom of the steps leading up to the hotel.

'I'll see you at breakfast.'

He gave her a light kiss on the cheek and Chloe was pleased to find it gave her not the slightest thrill.

She collected her key from the desk and went up the wide staircase to her room.

Mrs Keeling was next door and there was a shared bathroom between them. Very quietly, in case the woman was asleep, Chloe let herself into the bathroom and silently edged open the door into her employer's bedroom.

Voices stopped her in her tracks.

'Someone like Chloe would be perfect for him,' Mrs Keeling was saying. 'I wonder how we could bring it about?'

'Benedict prefers buxom brunettes like Magda.' That was Olivia.

Chloe silently closed the door, but not before hearing the older woman say, 'We don't want anything like that again.'

Chloe's cheeks flamed. They were talking about her and Benedict! She was glad she had heard no more before she closed the door.

She sat on the edge of her bed, breathing slowly to steady herself and willing the colour to go from her cheeks. Then she opened her bedroom door and closed it more noisily, as if she'd just come in. She let herself into the bathroom again, tapped on Mrs Keeling's door and went in.

'There you are, dear. Have you had a nice evening?'

'Lovely. A beautiful meal and the most unusual cabaret.'

She told them all about the restaurant and the snake charmer and the dancer.

'You look very flushed,' Olivia commented. 'I hope Benedict didn't give you too much wine. You don't want a headache for travelling tomorrow.'

'No. I had very little,' Chloe hastily assured her. 'It's just very warm in the hotel.' She turned to Mrs Keeling. 'Is there anything I can do for you?'

Mrs Keeling patted her hand. 'Nothing, dear. Run along and get some sleep. You look pretty in your new dress. Did Benedict notice it? I'm sure he did.'

'He said he liked it,' said Chloe shyly.

Mrs Keeling nodded in a satisfied way and Chloe bade them both good night and left the room quickly before there could be any more comments about Benedict.

In her room, she undressed and was soon in bed. She hoped Mrs Keeling wouldn't be too disappointed but she had no intention of becoming Benedict's girlfriend. She didn't think Benedict wanted it either.

She snuggled under the soft blankets, wrapped her arms around her shoulders and imagined herself in the taxi, close to Adam. He loved her, there was no doubt of that now. If only he would say it. Well, she would have to see what she could do about it.

She'd telephone him soon and arrange another meeting.

She yawned, and in a few minutes was fast asleep.

# A Mystery

Betty's arrival at Hampdens, two weeks after the family's return from London, enlivened the whole household. She talked gardens with Mrs Keeling, revealing a knowledge of the subject which Chloe had never suspected. She admired the raised beds which Mrs Keeling carefully tended and, on her first day there, the two of them sat in the garden after breakfast and discussed plant catalogues for most of the morning.

She enthused over Mrs Foster's cakes and begged for some recipes, which pleased the housekeeper greatly.

'She is much like Magda in her looks,' said Mrs Keeling, 'but she is nothing like her in any other way.'

Benedict, too, might have seen some resemblance because, unusually, he seemed always to be around the house instead of in his studio as he normally would have been.

He took all his meals with them and gazed at Betty across the table when he thought she wasn't looking. Mrs Keeling and Chloe noticed this and exchanged amused glances.

After dinner that first evening of her stay, Betty and Chloe went out into the garden where they could sit and talk without being overheard.

Although it was now well into autumn, the evenings were still warm, and Betty breathed in deeply of the soft scented air as they strolled in the grounds.

'You are so lucky to live in this beautiful place,' she said enviously. 'Are you pleased you came?'

'Of course. I love it here, but I miss you and . . . ' She paused.

'And Adam?'

Chloe smiled sadly at her friend. 'What am I to do about him? Is he still seeing Susannah after that row? He seems afraid to stand up to Dr Blaine.'

'Actually I have some news about

Adam,' said Betty mysteriously. 'Let's sit down and I'll tell you.'

'He told me this in strict confidence, but he said I could tell you. It's about Susannah.'

Chloe looked at her friend in alarm, a sinking feeling in her heart. Strict confidence and Susannah? Not another secret engagement, surely?

'Don't look so stricken,' said Betty. 'It should cheer you up. He and Susannah didn't see each other for a while after the row, then one day he bumped into her by chance in town. She was looking very unhappy. She was with a man who left as soon as Adam spoke to her. She begged Adam to talk to her, so he took her for lunch.'

Chloe looked at her friend intently, but said nothing.

'It seems that Susannah has a secret love,' Betty went on. 'They've been seeing each other for months. Her father would go mad if he found out. The man is respectable and has money but he's married — unhappily, so

Susannah said. He plans to get a divorce and marry Susannah when she's twenty-one, which is next year.'

'So she's not interested in Adam?'

'She never was. She was just showing off at the surgery and, of course, it put people off the scent of this other man. She's besotted with him.'

'Adam tried to make her see how her father would feel, and what other people would think, but she wouldn't listen. Adam's very annoyed with her. He feels she's used him — and caused him to lose you.'

'What did she want Adam to do? Did she think he could persuade Dr Blaine to see things her way?'

'No. She just wanted to talk to someone.'

Chloe looked thoughtful. 'I see.'

'There's something else you should know,' Betty went on. 'Adam's brother is a doctor in America . . . '

'I know,' said Chloe.

'Well, did you also know that he's been writing to Adam suggesting that he should join him and set up a joint practice over there?'

Chloe's brow furrowed. 'When I met him in London, Adam said he'd been to the American Embassy — but he didn't mention going to America.'

'He wouldn't. It might have influenced you. He wants you to come to him because you love him, not because of something which sounds like blackmail.'

'Yet he told you about it?'

'I don't think he meant to. It was just that once he started to talk, it all came out in a flood. He does love you, Chloe.'

'But what can I do? I can't leave here now. Mrs Keeling depends on me, and Olivia trusts me to look after her mother. Perhaps I should never have come.'

'That was my fault,' said Betty miserably. 'I found the advertisement and encouraged you to apply for it.'

'Don't be silly. The decision was mine. Don't blame yourself.'

'I wish I could do something about it,' said Betty.

On the second morning of Betty's visit, Chloe was in Mrs Keeling's room, helping her to bathe and dress, when the old lady announced that she was staying in bed that day.

'Staying in bed? Are you feeling ill?' Chloe asked in alarm. 'Let me take your temperature.'

'You don't need to take my temperature. I'm not ill, I'm just a little tired and have decided I shall stay in bed for a few hours.'

Chloe studied her. She didn't look ill. On the other hand, they'd all stayed up quite late the night before, talking and playing cards, and it was possible she *was* feeling tired.

'Very well. Mrs Foster can bring you a light breakfast and then I'll come and sit with you.'

Mrs Keeling looked indignant. 'You'll

do no such thing! You and Betty will go out for a drive around the Cotswolds. You'll have lunch out and come back at tea-time.'

Chloe gave her an accusing look. 'You don't feel tired, do you? You just want me to have a day out with Betty.' She sat on the side of the bed. 'You're being very naughty. I can't go out for the day and leave you.'

'You can leave me in bed. I'll be fine here. Mrs Foster will keep an eye on me.'

'Oh, dear,' said Chloe. 'I really don't know what to do.'

There was a knock at the bedroom door, then Benedict popped his head into the room.

'Ah, just the person.' Mrs Keeling beckoned him in. 'I'm feeling tired and want to spend a few hours in bed. Can you please tell this young lady that it would be quite all right for her to take Betty for a drive and let me have a rest.'

Benedict looked from one to the other.

'A battle of wills, is it? Of course it will be all right. I'll keep an eye on you. I'll peep in every hour on the hour. How's that?' he asked Chloe.

Chloe gave in. 'It *would* be nice to have a day out with Betty,' she admitted. 'I'm longing to show her around the lovely countryside. Thank you both. We won't be late back.'

'I've already telephoned Sam,' said Mrs Keeling with an impish smile. 'He'll be at the door in half an hour.'

★　★　★

'Which would you consider the most beautiful village in the Cotswolds, Sam?' Chloe asked as they settled themselves in the car.

Sam considered. 'That's a hard one, that is. What about the one they call The Venice of the Cotswolds?'

'That sounds rather grand,' said Chloe.

'It's only called that because of the water. It isn't grand but it is very pretty.'

'Is it far?'

'In a straight line from here, not very far; but Mrs Keeling said you were to have a tour, so we won't go there in a straight line. I'll show you the country-side on the way.'

'Sounds lovely.' Betty snuggled back into the corner of the seat and they set off.

It was a beautiful sunny autumn day. Sunlight slanted through the trees and threw deep shadows across the fields. Dry-stone walls ran for miles, edging the roads and crossing the pastures where fat, woolly sheep cropped the grass, pausing only for a moment to look up at the passing car before returning to their meal.

'Mrs Keeling told me that this has been a wool area for hundreds of years. Great houses and abbeys and churches were built with the proceeds from the sale of the wool,' Chloe told Betty.

They drove on through tiny villages where sleepy cats snoozed on garden walls, and down narrow lanes made narrower by thick hedges and greenery that overflowed on either side.

'I can understand why you love it here,' said Betty. 'It's timeless.'

'It is. Soft and timeless.'

'Nearly there,' said Sam. 'Another two miles.'

As soon as they entered the village they understood the reason for its name.

A very pretty, narrow and winding river meandered through it, crossed at intervals by elegant stone bridges.

'Bourton-on-the-Water,' said Sam. 'Isn't it beautiful?'

'Look at the little shops,' enthused Betty. 'Do let's explore.'

'We'll be here for about three hours,' Chloe told Sam. 'Go and get a drink and some food if you like.'

'Why don't we have an early lunch ourselves?' suggested Betty. 'Let's try the hotel over there.'

They crossed a stone bridge, stopping in the middle to watch the ducks passing underneath and reappearing on the other side.

'I wish I had some bread for them,' said Chloe.

The bridges were very picturesque; low arches, with just a slightly raised edge at either side.

They walked over the river and then strolled along a grassy path to the hotel.

'Let's sit in the window where we can see the water,' suggested Betty.

They chose a simple lunch, mindful of Mrs Foster's dinners.

'But I must have some gateau,' said Betty. 'It looks so creamy.'

'You're like Adam,' said Chloe. 'He loves creamy sweets.' She looked at Betty in dismay. 'Bother — I wasn't going to talk about him!'

'Did you think about what I told you last night?'

'I did. I couldn't get to sleep for thinking about it. Does he really mean it — about America?'

'If I were you, I wouldn't risk it,' said Betty decisively. 'Why don't you ask to see him again?'

'What good will that do? It would

just unsettle me again and he's told me in no uncertain terms that he won't make a commitment.'

Betty frowned. 'I'll never forgive myself if you two don't get together.'

'Wait a few weeks, then perhaps I'll see him,' said Chloe.

'A few weeks may be too late,' Betty warned.

Their gateaux arrived and Betty's attention was diverted by the confection of sponge cake, strawberries and cream. Chloe took the opportunity to change the subject.

'How do you like Benedict? He seems to like you — very much!'

Betty blushed. 'I think he's very nice. He's promised to show me his drawings in the studio tomorrow.'

'Not his etchings?' teased her friend.

'I wonder why he isn't married?' Betty asked. 'He must be quite a catch.'

Chloe told her the story of Magda.

Betty looked thoughtful. 'He visits France quite often?'

'Yes — but he has a French publisher.'

'Hmm. Maybe he does, but it suggested something else to me — or rather, some*one* else.'

'Do you mean he goes to see Magda?' asked Chloe.

'It's possible. His mother wouldn't know. You say he's very secretive about his private life.'

'Then you'll have to work extra hard to attract him.'

'I have enough trouble with *your* love life,' Betty countered. 'I haven't time for one of my own!'

Chloe stood up. 'Come on. If we sit here much longer we'll have no time to explore the village.'

On the following afternoon, Benedict drove the girls and his mother to a tennis party at the nearby home of some friends. Mrs Keeling was settled in a comfortable chair in the shade with several other elderly ladies while Chloe and Betty went off with Benedict to make up sets to play mixed doubles.

Most of the young people of the neighbourhood had been invited, but Chloe and Betty, as strangers, became the subject of great interest among the young men.

Chloe was amused to see that Benedict kept a firm hold of Betty's arm and managed to avoid playing with anyone else.

It was another sunny day and tea was served in the garden. Chloe helped herself to a selection of sandwiches and little sausage rolls and took her plate to a bench near Mrs Keeling.

'Where are Betty and Benedict?' the old lady asked.

'I'm not sure — they've disappeared. I expect they've gone to look at the garden.'

Particularly the privacy of the shrubbery, thought Chloe, thinking of Benedict's face as he'd looked at Betty.

As she spoke, the missing pair appeared from round a hedge behind her. Their faces were flushed, but it might simply have been due to the sun.

'All alone?' asked Benedict. 'I'll have to find you a companion, Chloe.'

'Please don't,' she protested hastily. 'I'm quite happy talking to your mother.'

He went off to get some food and Betty slid on to the bench beside her friend.

'Having a nice time?' Chloe asked.

'Wonderful.' Betty's face was shining. 'Are we playing any more tennis?'

'I don't think so. We're leaving after tea. Several people have gone already.

And Mrs Keeling is looking tired.'

Betty swallowed her disappointment and gave Benedict a wide smile as he returned with a plate of sandwiches for her.

'Guess where we're going tomorrow evening?' Betty said to Chloe. 'Actually, you'll never guess, so I'll tell you. Benedict is taking me to the pictures to see Charlie Chaplin in *The Gold Rush*. It's supposed to be ever so funny.'

Chloe decided not to remind her that she'd said she was giving up the pictures for ever after Valentino died.

'You must come with us,' said Benedict hastily.

'And play gooseberry? Thank you very much, but I don't think so. You two go with my blessing.'

Well, one romance is progressing satisfactorily, she thought to herself.

⋆   ⋆   ⋆

After dinner, they all sat in the drawing-room reading quietly.

'All that fresh air has made me very sleepy,' said Mrs Keeling, yawning.

The two girls agreed, and immediately yawned widely themselves.

'This is an interesting book,' said Chloe. '*The Cotswolds In The Last Century*. I love these old sepia photographs. Look at this one of Bourton-on-the-Water.'

She handed the book to Betty, and as she did so, a photograph slid from between the pages and fluttered to the floor.

Chloe stooped to pick it up. It showed a wide-eyed little girl, with dark hair tied at the sides of her head in bunches.

'Oh, goodness! It's Milly Moppet!' she cried.

'What?' Benedict jumped up and almost snatched the photograph from her hand.

She stared at him in surprise and he had the grace to blush.

'I'm sorry,' said Benedict. 'I'd lost it. I wondered where it was.' He slipped the photograph hastily into his jacket pocket. 'I think I'll go up to the studio and finish some work.'

He kissed his mother goodnight, waved to the girls, and left the room.

Chloe and Betty looked at each other, Chloe raising her eyebrows eloquently.

'It *was* Milly Moppet,' she whispered. 'A photograph of Milly Moppet.'

Tiredness shortly overcame Mrs Keeling, and Chloe took her upstairs and helped her into bed.

When she returned to the drawing-room, Betty was sitting in an armchair with her eyes closed and Chloe thought at first that she had fallen asleep.

'I'm thinking,' Betty announced. 'Have you read any books by Agatha Christie? She has a Belgian detective who reasons the solutions to his cases by means of his 'little grey cells'. I'm using my little grey cells.'

'And what is the solution?'

'Well — Benedict was in love with

Magda. Magda lives in France. Benedict visits France frequently. Milly Moppet looks decidedly French. What do you think?'

'That Milly Moppet is his and Magda's child.'

'Exactly. Though why he keeps quiet about it, I don't know.'

'Probably because his mother didn't like Magda,' said Chloe, 'and wouldn't like to think there was something between them.'

'Mm. I wonder whether we'll ever solve the case?' asked Betty.

'Not tonight for sure. I'm too sleepy!' Chloe stood up. 'I'm going to bed. Good night. See you in the morning.'

# Mrs Keeling's New Doctor

In due course, Betty returned home to Alderton, and everyone missed her cheerful presence. Chloe looked forward to a telephone call from her friend on that first Monday night, and the chance to gossip about their week together. However, when she answered the telephone, Betty's news came out in a rush.

'He's gone, Chloe! Adam! He's gone! Left, just like that, last week. You can imagine what sort of mood Dr Blaine is in.'

'Gone? But where? America?'

'No-one knows. Just like you, he didn't tell anyone.'

'Have you any ideas?' Chloe asked. 'He seems to have been confiding in you lately.' She couldn't help the accusing tone that edged her voice.

'No. Of course not. How should I

know where he is?'

But Betty seemed to be babbling and Chloe felt suddenly suspicious.

'Betty, you haven't told him where I am?'

'No! No! I promised, didn't I? How could you think I . . . '

'All right. I'm sorry. Look, I'll ring you again tomorrow, all right? I don't feel like chatting right now.'

She replaced the telephone and stood for a few minutes, thinking. If Betty had told Adam where she was, he would turn up soon and the last thing she wanted was a scene at Hampdens.

She went slowly up to her room.

Would it be best to tell Mrs Keeling the whole story? That way, if Adam did turn up, it would be less of a shock.

Undecided, she went to bed, but tossed and turned for most of the night.

The next morning, Chloe was very quiet. Mrs Keeling regarded her anxiously for a while, then at last she asked, 'Are you feeling quite well, Chloe?'

Chloe looked at her, unsure how to answer.

'If you don't mind my saying so, you look as if you have a problem, dear,' Mrs Keeling went on. 'Can I help in any way?'

Chloe was silent for a few minutes then she took a deep breath and said, 'I would like to talk to you, if I may.'

'Of course. Let's go into the drawing-room. There's a fire in there and we can forget this nasty weather.' She glanced towards the windows where a strong wind was blowing sharp gusts of rain against the glass.

'That's the trouble with the Cotswolds

weather — it can be very wet and gusty.'

They settled themselves by the fire and she looked expectantly at Chloe.

Hesitantly at first, then in a stronger voice, Chloe told her all about her relationship with Adam, about her hurt at his failure to declare his love, though she was sure he felt it, and about Susannah.

Mrs Keeling considered. 'So you thought you would run away from him? Probably hoping all the time that he would come looking for you?'

Chloe nodded.

'Did you consider that removing yourself from the scene might have propelled him into Susannah's arms?'

'But she loves someone else!'

'Ah, but you didn't know that at the time.'

Chloe stared into the fire.

'So you think I did the wrong thing in leaving Alderton?' she asked at last.

Mrs Keeling smiled. 'You did absolutely the right thing as far as I'm concerned, but that is my own purely selfish view.'

Chloe smiled back. 'I'm glad I came. I love it here. But I can't think what to do about Adam.'

'And now he's disappeared.'

'So Betty says. That's why I'm telling you all about it. If he has found out where I am, he may turn up here.'

'From what you tell me about him, I don't think he'll do anything silly. He'll just want to talk to you.'

'What do you think I should do?'

'Oh, Chloe, my dear.' Mrs Keeling took her hand. 'I can't tell you what to do. It's your life. But if you love him, then you must listen to what he has to say and give him time to make up his mind. He sounds a very serious and a very ambitious young man. But you can't rush him. Just give him time. If you really love him, it will be worth waiting for him.'

Life went on quietly. Betty had no news of Adam and he did not appear at Hampdens.

Chloe decided that he must have gone to America after all. Perhaps he would write.

She kept herself busy so that she had little time to brood about him.

One evening, Benedict took both her and his mother to a concert at the local church. Rosalyn was in the choir and performed two solos. Her voice was sweet and clear, quite at odds with her tomboyish appearance. They all felt very proud of her.

'A young woman of talent,' said Benedict. 'A gardener, a motorcyclist and now a singer. Do you think it's spending so much time in the fresh air that does it?'

Rosalyn had tried to persuade Chloe

to join the choir, but without success.

'Acting was enough of a problem,' she said. 'I definitely can't sing.'

Chloe and Mrs Keeling took to visiting the surrounding villages in their quest for new places for coffee or lunch and Chloe began to feel she was getting to know the area really well.

In the afternoons, she obeyed the doctor's orders and walked Mrs Keeling, well wrapped up, round the garden paths.

Autumn was well advanced now. Rainy, windy days became more frequent. The two of them often pulled a little table close to the fire and pored together over jigsaw puzzles or worked at tapestry pictures. It was a pleasant time for them both.

'Wait till the snow comes,' said Benedict. 'It hangs about for ages. Some villages are cut off for days. There's a story that in the sixteen hundreds, the snow hung around until August.'

'I wouldn't mind,' said Chloe. 'I love snow. And we shall be very cosy here, I'm sure.'

One morning as Chloe was dressing, there came a hasty knocking at her bedroom door.

'Miss Perle, Miss Perle. Come quickly!'

It was Mrs Foster and she sounded very frightened.

'It's Mrs Keeling. I don't like the look of her at all.'

Chloe rushed to Mrs Keeling's bedroom. The old lady was grey in the face and breathing heavily. She gripped Chloe's hand.

'Pain,' she said. 'In my chest.'

'Quickly,' said Chloe to the housekeeper, who was standing trembling at her side. 'Go and telephone for Dr Marchant. Say it's urgent.'

Chloe placed a pillow under the old lady's legs, then sat by the bed and stroked her hands.

It seemed ages, but in reality it was only about ten minutes later that she heard Mrs Foster open the front door and greet the doctor.

By now, Benedict, summoned by Mrs Foster, had joined Chloe at his mother's bedside. He went down to greet the doctor and Chloe heard the quiet rumble of men's voices.

'In here, Doctor,' she heard Benedict say as he came back upstairs.

Chloe looked up just as he came into the room — and behind him strode Adam Raven.

She felt the colour drain from her face as he looked at her, but the look was brief; he was concentrating on his patient.

Chloe left the room and went to find Mrs Foster.

'Where's Dr Marchant?'

'He's ill, Miss. In hospital himself. This young man is his locum. Dr Raven his name is. Never seen him before, but he seems very nice.' Mrs Foster was filling the kettle as she spoke. 'Do you think he'd like a cup of tea?'

'I'm sure he will, Mrs Foster.'

Chloe returned to the bedroom to see Adam washing his hands at the bowl in the corner of the room. Benedict had rejoined them and Mrs Keeling already looked more relaxed.

'She won't need to go to hospital,' Adam was saying. 'It was a slight attack of angina pectoris. A few days' rest and she'll be as right as rain. Make sure she stays in bed, Nurse, and does nothing. I'll pop in tomorrow and see how she is.'

'I'll see you out, Doctor,' said Benedict.

With another quick glance at Chloe, Adam left the room and she heard the two men making their way downstairs.

Silently she moved to the window. Adam was getting into his car. He looked up at her but made no sign.

'I can't believe it,' Chloe whispered to herself. 'He's here in Cheston Parva.'

Mrs Keeling moved and Chloe returned to her side, still in a state of shock after seeing Adam and moving like an automaton. But Adam would have to wait; for now, she had to make sure Mrs Keeling was well looked after.

But he's coming again tomorrow, she thought, and her heart lifted involuntarily. Perhaps we'll talk then.

After dinner, Olivia arrived at the house, looking worried.

Chloe hastened to reassure her.

'She'll be fine. The doctor said a few days' rest in bed and she'll be quite well.'

'Dr Marchant?'

'No. He's in hospital himself apparently. It was his locum, Dr Raven.'

Olivia looked worried. 'Did he seem — competent?' she asked.

'Oh, he's very good,' said Chloe quickly, then, as Olivia gave her a puzzled look, she added, 'He's calling tomorrow, so you'll be able to speak to him yourself.'

* * *

Adam called again the next morning, but there was still no opportunity for Chloe to speak to him on her own. This time, both Olivia and Benedict were in the room when he examined their mother, and it was Olivia who saw him out. He gave Chloe an agonised look as he left the room.

Olivia came back upstairs and said, 'Well, he seems very nice, I must say. And he says Mother is doing well. In fact, she can probably get up tomorrow.'

She looked at Chloe. 'You haven't been out for a day or two, have you?'

'No. But that doesn't matter. I'll go out when Mrs Keeling is better.'

'You'll go out now,' Olivia countered. 'You should get some fresh air. I'm sure you can find something to do in the village.'

'Well, if you think you can manage,' said Chloe. 'I would like to see whether a book I ordered has come in yet.'

'Off you go, then,' said Olivia, 'and don't hurry back.'

In her bedroom, Chloe studied her reflection in the mirror.

Most girls had had their hair cropped very short so that they could wear the cloche hats which were so very popular at the moment. Chloe loved the hats — but she also loved her hair and hadn't wanted to cut it too short.

Now, she pulled on her hat over her fashionable bob.

The day was dry, but she took a small umbrella just in case of rain, and she wore the new warm tweed coat with a wide fur collar which she'd bought in Bath on a shopping expedition with Mrs Keeling. The cream hat with the brown ribbon went well with it.

Outside it was breezy and there were ominous clouds gathering overhead. Chloe walked briskly, enjoying being out in the fresh air.

The walk to the village took about twenty minutes along a country road, with nowhere to shelter if the rain started, but once she reached the village, there were shops where she could take refuge if need be.

As she walked, she thought of the coincidence of Adam being Dr Marchant's locum. But she knew it wasn't coincidence. Somehow, Adam had managed to discover where she was and had obtained the position deliberately.

The road was deserted. Occasionally a car passed.

If only Adam would drive past and see her. How could she contrive a meeting?

She was still deliberating on this when she came to the first houses on the edge of the village and turned into the main street.

Cheston Parva was lucky in having a small book shop. Chloe had ordered a book on the identification of birds and went inside to see if it had arrived. The book was part of her plan for new interests for Mrs Keeling, who spent much of her time on her day-bed looking out into the garden.

The bird population was large and varied and Chloe thought that their identification would prove an interesting hobby. The book was to be a surprise.

However, the shopkeeper was apologetic.

'No news of it yet, I'm afraid,' he said. 'Perhaps in a few days?'

Disappointed, she left the shop.

She decided to buy a new pair of stockings and went into the haberdashers. She would have loved to wear silk stockings but the price was prohibitive, so she settled for artificial silk, as usual, and bought two pairs.

By the time she came out, the rain had begun to fall. Large black spots were quickly darkening the pavement.

Struggling to put up her small umbrella, she looked around for shelter and decided to aim for The Mob Cap tearoom until the rain passed over.

'Chloe! I thought it was you. What are you doing here?'

It was Benedict. Good. If he had his car, she wouldn't get wet going home, she thought.

'I was going to take shelter in the tearoom over there,' she said. 'This rain looks as if it's going to be heavy.'

'Good idea, I'll come with you. Give me the umbrella, I'll hold it up.'

She surrendered the handle and Benedict tried to position the small canopy so that it covered both of them.

'Perhaps if we walk very close together?' he suggested.

He put an arm round her waist and pulled her to him. She began to laugh and he joined in as they made awkward progress to the teashop.

A man tried to pass them on the narrow pavement and there was a collision. Benedict apologised, and as he moved the umbrella to one side, Chloe saw that the man was Adam.

In a few seconds, Adam had taken in the fact that Chloe had someone's arm round her waist and was being held close. Sparks seemed to fly from his eyes as he looked at her.

Confused, she said nothing as Benedict hurried her into the tearoom.

'Was that the new doctor?' he asked, as he helped her remove her wet coat. 'His hat was pulled so well down, I couldn't be sure.'

'I . . . I think so.'

'How odd! He looked very bad-tempered, almost as if he was furious with you. He glared at you. You don't know him, do you?' He looked at her curiously.

'How — how should I know him?' she stammered.

He shrugged. 'He's a doctor, you're a nurse. You might have met before somewhere.'

'Oh, don't let's talk about him.' Chloe looked around for a waitress. 'I need some tea to warm me up.'

As Benedict gave their order, she looked out of the window at the rain that was now falling heavily, her thoughts spinning. Three times recently she'd seen Adam, yet each and every time she'd been unable to speak to him. She should have simply introduced him to Benedict as an old friend when they'd passed in the street, but then, how could they have talked in front of a third party?

And now she had denied knowing him at all! This would certainly lead to further complications.

Her reflections were interrupted by the arrival of the tea. She busied herself with the pot while Benedict watched her.

'I'm sure the doctor was annoyed with you,' he said.

'For goodness' sake!' Chloe was irritated. 'Why should he be? Do you think he felt I shouldn't have come out and left your mother?'

'It would hardly be his place to think things like that. And he would know that you would only leave her if someone else was with her.'

There was silence as they drank their tea.

Chloe glanced out of the window again.

'I believe the rain has stopped,' she commented.

'It doesn't matter. I'll take you home anyway. I have to visit Annabel, but I can take you home first.'

'Please, don't bother,' she protested, standing up and allowing him to help her into her coat. 'The sky's quite clear now. I should like the walk.'

'Are you quite sure?'

'Quite. I came out to get some air and exercise.'

She set off in the direction of Hampdens. The rain had brought a freshness to the air and she breathed deeply, relishing the just-washed tang of it all.

A car passed her and stopped several yards in front. A man climbed out and came towards her. Adam.

They looked at each other without speaking. Then his arms went round her and he held her close.

For a moment she stood, her eyes closed, locked in his arms. Then she pulled away.

'Someone might see us . . . '

'Get in the car. We can talk there.'

'No, I must get back. I can't be away too long.'

'But we must talk. I need to explain.' His expression was anxious.

'You have a great deal to explain,' she agreed. 'I can't imagine how you come to be here.'

'Can you get away tonight? We could have dinner?' he pressed.

She hesitated. Olivia would be with her mother and wouldn't mind Chloe having an evening off. But she didn't want to ask for time off when Mrs Keeling was unwell . . .

Regretfully she shook her head. 'That's not possible. But . . . ' She hesitated.

'Yes?'

'At the far end of the garden at Hampdens, there's a little summerhouse. I could meet you there at, say, half-past nine? Mrs Keeling will be asleep by then. I'll say I need some fresh air.'

'All right. But how do I reach it? I can hardly stroll in through the garden.'

'A hundred yards down the lane at the side of the house there's a little path running alongside the garden hedge. Follow that and you'll see the summer-house. There's a gate in the hedge.'

He smiled. 'I'll be there. Now let me take you home.'

'No. I might be seen in your car. People will talk. I'll see you this evening.'

She pressed his hand and hurried away.

★   ★   ★

On her return, Chloe was pleased to find that Mrs Keeling was feeling much better and talking of getting up and dressing the next day.

The woman was interested to hear that Chloe and Benedict had taken shelter from the rain together.

'You two would make a lovely couple,' she said wistfully. 'But I think you've lost him to your friend, Betty.'

Chloe smiled. '*They* make a lovely couple.'

The old lady nodded. 'If Benedict doesn't want you, then I'll settle for

Betty,' she said. 'I had a charming letter from her this morning. I hope she'll come to stay again soon.'

Chloe had had a letter from Betty, too.

*'I may have to find somewhere else to live in the near future,' she had written. 'Gerald, my cousin, has inherited a hotel near Bournemouth. He already runs a small hotel; this is much bigger. He has suggested to Aunt Ellen that she goes to live there so that he can keep an eye on her. Of course, she likes the idea of being with her son and living near the sea. But where does that leave poor little me? Perhaps I'll find a living-in position like you.'*

The letter didn't mention Adam. She had a guilty conscience, Chloe thought. Betty had told him where to find the other girl, she know she had. But why, when she'd promised faithfully to say nothing?

After dinner, she read to Mrs Keeling

for an hour from her favourite novel, Jane Austen's *Emma*.

'You're like Emma,' she said to the old lady as she finally tucked her in for the night. 'Your favourite occupation is matchmaking.'

'Ah, but with one crucial difference: Emma wasn't very successful, whereas *I* shall do better. When I meet your Adam, I shall help *your* romance along.'

Chloe longed to say that she had met Adam twice already, but having kept silent regarding his identity so far, she didn't know how to broach the subject. Instead, she drew the bedroom curtains and quietly said good night before leaving the bedroom and closing the door.

She went to her own room, applied a dusting of powder to her face and smoothed her hair. These preparations complete, she listened outside Mrs Keeling's door. Hearing no sound she made her way downstairs to the drawing-room.

'I'm going into the garden for some

air,' she told Olivia. 'Everything is quiet in Mrs Keeling's room.'

She hurried through the garden. The smell of woodsmoke from a bonfire hung on the air. All traces of the rain had vanished. It was a fine evening.

Adam was waiting at the summerhouse.

'This is like a nineteenth-century novel,' he said. 'A secret assignation in a summerhouse!'

He was sitting on a long couch, but Chloe settled in a basket chair opposite. They didn't touch. There was a formality between them which wouldn't soften until questions had been asked and answered.

'Have you left Dr Blaine's surgery for good?' Chloe asked.

'Yes. But this is just a temporary appointment until Dr Marchant returns.'

'So how did you find me? Did Betty tell you?'

He nodded and she frowned.

'I'm very annoyed with her for breaking her promise to keep my whereabouts secret.'

'Aren't you glad to see me?'

Chloe said nothing but looked down at the floor.

'Chloe, aren't you glad to see me — just a little?'

'You know I am. But why did Betty break her promise?'

'She was afraid I was going to join my brother in America. She thought that we . . . that we were meant to be together.'

Chloe continued to stare at the floor.

'But she didn't tell me where you were, not in so many words,' he went on. 'She came into my consulting room one morning and put a magazine on my desk. You know, the magazine which contained the advertisement for your post here? She said, 'Read that — there's something of interest to you in there,' and then marched out.

'That evening, I read it from cover to cover. I knew as soon as I came to that advertisement that I'd found you.'

'How did you get the locum position?'

'Pure luck. I called on Dr Marchant, the local physician, to ask if he knew of any vacant positions in the area and it so happened that he was going into hospital and needed someone himself. It couldn't have worked out better.'

'Agatha Christie could use you in one of her books,' Chloe observed wryly.

Adam started to laugh and, with a sense of release, she laughed with him. Then he got to his feet and pulled her on to the couch beside him. His arms slid round her and he held her close.

'I've got something to tell you,' he whispered.

She raised her face to his. 'What?'

'I love you. I love you. I love you.'

She made no protest when he pressed his lips to hers, and returned his kiss with an enthusiasm which surprised and delighted him.

'Am I correct in thinking that you feel the same way?'

'Can you doubt it?' she answered.

Two kisses later, she slipped from his arms.

'I must go. Mrs Keeling may wake up and need me.'

She smoothed down her skirt.

'Am I tidy? I'm supposed to have been walking in the garden.'

'I wish you could stay longer,' he said, 'but I'll see you in the morning when I call on my patient. Shall you tell them about us?'

'Not yet. Let's wait a while. Now I must go.'

She gave him a quick kiss and fled down the path to the house.

# A Surprise Visitor

Adam arrived at the house after breakfast the next morning and declared Mrs Keeling well enough to resume her regular activities.

'I know I'm leaving you in good hands,' he told her, smiling at Chloe.

'She's a treasure,' said Mrs Keeling. 'I don't know how I should manage without her.'

'I'll see Dr Raven out,' said Chloe, and led the way downstairs.

At the door, Adam stopped and asked her, 'What exactly is the relationship between you and the man I met you with yesterday?'

'Benedict? There's no relationship. He's Mrs Keeling's son. He lives here.'

'Lives here? So you see him every day?'

'Most days.'

Adam looked away from her across the garden.

'He's not the reason you refused to see me?' he asked, jealousy sharpening his tone.

Chloe caught his arm. 'Adam, there is nothing between Benedict and me. There never was, there never will be. He's in love with Betty.'

He turned and looked at her in amazement. 'Betty?'

'Yes. She came to stay here for a week and it was love at first sight. At least, Mrs Keeling and I hope it was. They certainly became very close.'

'Oh, Chloe, you don't know how happy it makes me to hear you say that.'

She looked up into his eyes. 'I love you and only you.' She kissed him quickly. 'Off you go. I have work to do and you must have patients to see.'

'I'll see you soon?'

'Soon.' She was happy to see him walk away from her with a spring in his step.

★  ★  ★

That evening, as Chloe sat with Benedict in the drawing-room, he laid aside his book and looked at her.

'Chloe, I don't think you've been quite honest with me.'

She started guiltily. 'What do you mean?'

'You said you didn't know Dr Raven.'

She made no comment.

'Yet I passed the house this morning as you were saying goodbye to him at the front door, and it didn't remotely look like you don't know him!' he said meaningfully, and he didn't need to say any more. She knew by the look on his face at what moment he had passed.

'Very well. Everyone will know soon anyway. Yes, I do know Dr Raven. I worked with him at the surgery in Alderton.'

'You seemed to know him rather well.'

Her head came up. Was this a criticism?

'We're in love,' she admitted quietly, and her pulse soared at the thought.

He looked at her without speaking, then he said, 'It all seems rather odd. You come here, then he appears. First you say you don't know him, then, two days later, you say you're in love!'

'What right have you to demand explanations?' she flared. 'I'm employed by your mother. I do my job well. Why should you expect to know all about my private life?'

He left his chair and moved across the room to sit next to her on the couch and took her hand.

'Chloe, I'm sorry. I'm not demanding anything. But in the time you've been here, I've become very fond of you. We all have. I would hate to see anyone take advantage of you. If you love him and he truly loves you, then I'm happy for you. I only want your happiness. Honestly. Friends?'

'Of course.' She gave him a shy smile. 'I'm sorry. I'm just a bit sensitive about it all. I will tell you the whole story — but I would like you to keep it to yourself for the time being. Please?'

'Of course.'

For the next ten minutes Benedict sat in silence as Chloe related how she had met Adam; how they had been attracted to each other; how Adam felt he couldn't commit himself to anyone until he had made his way in the world; how she had left her job and how he had discovered where she was living.

'And last night, he told me that he loves me,' she said quietly.

'So what will happen now?' he asked.

'We've only had half an hour together since he found me — no time for discussions. But it doesn't matter.' She gave him a radiant smile. 'He loves me. That's all that matters.'

A ring at the doorbell made them both jump.

'Mrs Foster's out. I'll go,' said Benedict.

Chloe listened to the voices at the front door. She could hear Benedict, a woman's voice, and the excited squeals of a child. Puzzled, she waited.

Benedict reappeared in the doorway

of the drawing-room holding a small girl of about five by the hand. She had large chocolate-brown eyes and dark hair tied in bunches on either side of her head.

Chloe stood up.

'Milly Moppet!'

The words were out before she realised she had spoken.

The little girl was clinging to Benedict and smiling up at him with a wide, happy grin.

'Chloe?' Benedict brought the child forward, looking down at her with pride. 'This is Madeleine, my daughter, usually called Milly. And Milly, this is my friend Chloe.'

The child made a tiny old-fashioned curtsey.

'*Bonsoir*, Chloe.'

'In English, please, Milly,' said her father.

Milly made a funny little shrug of her shoulders.

'Good evening, Chloe.'

The woman had remained standing

in the doorway but now Benedict turned and gestured to her.

'Magda, come and meet Chloe, my mother's nurse-companion and my friend.'

Chloe looked with interest at the woman who came forward to meet her. She was about her own age and elegantly dressed in an ankle-length, green velvet coat and high-heeled shoes. Her matching hat dipped pertly over one eye. She moved in a cloud of delicious scent.

'This is Magda, Milly's mother.'

The two young women shook hands before everyone sat down, with Milly perched on Benedict's lap.

'Chloe has just been telling me an interesting story,' Benedict said to Magda. 'Perhaps we had better tell her a story of our own?'

'Magda came to Cheston Parva six years ago, to improve her English,' he told Chloe. 'She was living with the family at the vicarage and became friendly with all the young people in the village. She and I were especially friendly.'

He smiled at Magda, but she looked uncomfortable.

'He wanted us to marry,' said Magda, 'but I, I think we are too young. So I go back to France.'

'And some months later, Milly was born.' Benedict gave his little daughter a kiss. 'But I knew nothing about her. It was two years before Magda wrote and told me that I had a daughter.'

'My mother say is not right he does not know. She wants us to marry. But I do not want to marry. And I do not want to live in England.'

'How did you manage to look after a child on your own?' asked Chloe.

'My mother and father help me. I work in hotel and they look after Madeleine. But now they are old. They say they cannot manage her on their own.'

Chloe looked at Benedict, puzzled.

'Magda has met someone whom she

*does* want to marry,' he said, with a twisted smile.

'He has much money,' said Magda, with a look of satisfaction. 'But he must travel abroad for many months each year and I can go with him. But not Madeleine. It is no life for a small girl. She cannot live with her *grandmére* and *grandpére*, so I think she will be happy with her father when I am away. Each time I return to France, she will come and live with me.'

She stroked the soft velvet of her coat as if delighted that she had arranged everything satisfactorily.

Chloe didn't know whether to approve of what seemed a sensible arrangement or to be horrified that a mother could leave her small child with so little emotion.

But Milly obviously adored her father. She was reaching up to pat his face and laughing as he pretended to bite her fingers. The child wouldn't be deprived of love if she stayed with Benedict.

But what about Mrs Keeling? She

knew nothing about Milly, the little girl who was her only grandchild. She was asleep upstairs knowing nothing of the drama below.

Chloe looked at Benedict. Had he forgotten his mother?

As if in answer to her thoughts, he smiled across at her.

'Chloe, do you think you could go upstairs and ask Olivia to join us? Don't tell her why — I'll explain to her.'

Olivia was in her mother's bedroom. Quietly Chloe gave her the message.

'I'm just going downstairs,' Olivia told Mrs Keeling. 'Benedict wants me. I'll be back in a moment.'

She gave Chloe a curious look as they descended the stairs, but to Chloe's relief, she asked no questions.

Olivia's face was a study when she entered the drawing-room and realised the identity of their visitor.

'Magda! It is Magda, isn't it?'

'It is. How are you, Olivia?'

The two women shook hands.

'And this is your little girl?'

Olivia smiled at Milly.

'This is *our* little girl,' Benedict corrected quietly.

Olivia sank down on the nearest chair.

'Good gracious!'

The story was related to her by her brother.

'I thought there was something,' she said when he'd finished. 'And Milly is the reason for your frequent visits to France?'

'The main reason,' he said.

'She's very sweet,' said Olivia. Then she voiced the concern that Chloe had been thinking. 'What about Mother?'

She and Benedict looked at each other in consternation.

'She always wanted a grandchild,' he said hopefully.

'But this is a strange way to get one,' said his sister. 'She'll have to be told at once. I'll go up now. Chloe, would you come with me?'

They went upstairs together.

Mrs Keeling was sitting up in bed finishing the cup of hot milk that Olivia had made for her.

'Could I hear voices downstairs? What did Benedict want?'

Olivia looked helplessly at Chloe, unsure how to broach the subject.

Chloe sat at the side of the bed and took the old lady's hand.

'Do you remember telling me about Benedict and Magda? How you thought there had been something serious between them, so serious that he couldn't settle down with another girl?'

'I'm sure there was.'

'Well, you were right. Benedict wanted to marry her but she didn't want marriage and she didn't want to live in England.'

'Why are you telling me this now? And how are you so sure?'

'Because Magda is downstairs,' said Olivia. 'She's come to see Benedict and she's brought . . . Mother, when Magda returned to France, she had Benedict's child.'

'Benedict's child!' Mrs Keeling looked at her in amazement.

'A little girl. Madeleine. Known as Milly,' said Chloe.

'Milly? You mean as in Milly Moppet, the little girl in his books?' 'Milly is Milly Moppet. She's his model. And she's so sweet,' said

Chloe.

Mrs Keeling stared into space. 'How could Benedict . . . ? I can't believe he . . . '

'Don't blame him, Mother. He was in love and probably desperate when he knew she was going back to France. Perhaps he thought that by . . . well, perhaps he thought it would influence her if . . . '

'That's all in the past,' said Chloe. 'We must think of the child.'

'My little granddaughter!' Mrs Keeling's lips trembled as she said it.

'My own little granddaughter! Oh, I must see her.'

'I'll tell Benedict to bring her up,' said Olivia.

'No. It might frighten her to come up and see me in bed. I'll come down and see her with everyone else.'

'It's too late for you to dress,' said Chloe firmly. 'You must put on your dressing gown and slippers. They'll understand.'

She picked up a hairbrush.

'Let me do your hair.'

Olivia went ahead to warn the others that Mrs Keeling was coming down and explained to Magda that she'd been ill recently.

Benedict whispered to Milly who looked towards the door with interest.

When Mrs Keeling appeared, Milly looked up at her father, excited but unsure of what was actually happening. 'This is a new *grandmere* for me? An English *grandmere*?'

Benedict gave her a kiss. 'Yes. Will you come and say hello to her?'

Milly nodded, crossed the room with her father and stood in front of Mrs Keeling.

'Hello, new Grandmother,' she said, with her funny little curtsey.

Mrs Keeling looked at her with tears running down her cheeks.

'You sweet little thing,' she said. 'My own little granddaughter.'

'Do not cry,' said Milly, and taking a tiny handkerchief from her pocket, handed it to her grandmother. 'Do not be sad.'

'I'm not sad. I'm so happy.'

Milly looked at her with her head on one side. 'I do not cry when I am happy.'

Mrs Keeling sat down on the couch and, unbidden, Milly climbed up beside her. Mrs Keeling smiled down at her, blinking through her tears.

Then, as if she had only just noticed her, she turned to the child's mother.

'Magda. I'm sorry. I was so thrilled with Milly.' She patted the child's knee. 'How are you? It is so long since we last met.'

They exchanged a few remarks but Mrs Keeling was obviously keen to concentrate on Milly who was now holding her hand.

'Mother?' Benedict had come to sit opposite her. 'Would you like Milly to live with us for part of the year?'

Mrs Keeling looked from him to Magda. 'But you didn't want to live in England,' she said to the French-woman.

'Not me. Just Madeleine,' she answered. 'I shall be abroad in different countries. It would not be suitable for a small child. I should like her to stay here with her Papa.'

Benedict tried to explain to his mother, whose attention was on the child.

'You will stay tonight,' Olivia said to Magda. 'I'll have a room prepared for you.'

'No.' Magda stood up, looking at her watch. 'My fianceé is calling back for me in five minutes. I cannot stay.'

'Mama!' Milly slid off the couch and ran to her mother, flinging her arms around her.

Magda bent and clasped the child in her arms, speaking soothingly to her in French. After a few minutes, Magda took her to Benedict who picked her up and held her close in his arms. Milly pressed her lips tightly together but did not cry.

As Magda left the room with Olivia, Milly buried her face in her father's neck.

'Poor little mite,' said her grandmother to Chloe. 'We must find lots of things for her to do so that she won't miss her mother. Tomorrow, you and Benedict must go up into the attic and find some toys for her to play with. There's a rocking horse and a pram and I'm sure we kept Olivia's dolls' house.'

Never mind watching the birds in the garden, thought Chloe, she has a wonderful new interest now.

\* \* \*

*So much has happened*, Chloe wrote to Betty, *but first I must forgive you for telling Adam, or rather, helping him to work out where I am. I have*

284

seen *him*, and the most wonderful thing is that he loves me! He told me so in a little summerhouse at the end of the garden. Could anything be more romantic?

We have been unable to meet long enough to make any plans for the future, but I don't mind. He loves me. That is enough for me for now.

The next important thing is that you were right about Benedict. He goes to France to see not Magda but his daughter! Yes, he has a little girl called Milly. She is the model for Milly Moppet. She is here with us now. Magda has gone abroad with her fiancé, leaving the child here until she returns.

Mrs Keeling, who has been ill lately but is better now, is so happy.

How is Aunt Ellen? When is she to move to Bournemouth? I hope . . . '

Milly was very subdued in the days that followed. Her grandmother and Chloe took her for car rides into the countryside, Benedict brought toys from the attic for her to play with, and Mrs Foster cooked the sort of meals which would appeal to a small appetite. But nothing could bring a smile to her face. She was polite and there were no tears, but it was easy to see that she was unhappy. She followed her father everywhere, making it difficult for him to concentrate on his work.

'She misses her mother,' said Mrs Keeling. 'She is very young to be separated from her. She knows Magda will return but the waiting is hard for her.'

There was no criticism of Magda. If she had stayed in France with her child, Mrs Keeling would never have had the pleasure of a grandchild. But it made her unhappy to see the little one so sad.

Chloe did her best to entertain Milly, but there was no natural affinity between her and the child.

Mrs Keeling looked at them as they sat together on the couch reading a Milly Moppet book.

'You two are complete opposites,' the old lady remarked. 'You are fair while Milly has dark hair and eyes like chocolate drops. Oh!' She clasped her hands together. 'I've got the solution.'

Chloe looked at her blankly.

'Betty!' exclaimed Mrs Keeling. 'Betty is very like Magda. Let's send for her and see if Milly takes to her. Go and telephone her now.'

'But I don't know whether she would be allowed any more time off,' Chloe protested.

'Ask her. Perhaps she could come for the weekend.'

As it turned out Betty was delighted to hear from Chloe, and was more than willing to accept her invitation.

She would ask Mary-Lou to do her Saturday morning dispensary duty and come for two days. She was eager to see the model for Milly Moppet.

Benedict motored down to get her and brought her back in triumph.

Mrs Keeling's intuition had been right; Betty's vivacity and resemblance to Magda ensured that Milly took to her at once. They became inseparable for the whole weekend.

'What about a visit to Annabel?' Benedict suggested that afternoon. 'Perhaps she would lend us Bubble and Squeak for a few hours.'

Milly looked puzzled. 'What is . . . Bubble and Squeak?'

He swung her up in his arms. 'Just wait till you see them. You'll love them.'

'But what are they?' she squealed as she was tickled.

But all that Benedict would say was, 'Wait and see.'

They piled into his car and half an hour later they were all sitting in Annabel's little sitting-room, drinking coffee and eating freshly-made short-bread. Milly, quite entranced, was sitting on the floor with the little dogs.

Chloe was pleased to see the little girl so relaxed and bubbly. Betty's visit was working wonders.

And Annabel was pleased to let Milly take the little dogs back to Hampdens for the afternoon.

'It will give me a chance to do some work in peace,' she said. 'Wear them out and they'll sleep all evening.'

Bubble and Squeak, used to the confines of a cottage garden, raced excitedly round the grounds at Hampdens.

Rosalyn had swept fallen leaves into a large pile at the end of the lawn. Now clouds of gold and brown leaves flew about as child and dogs demolished the mound.

'You'd better hide if Rosalyn comes,' Benedict warned. 'She'll shoot the boots off you!'

But Milly only laughed. Rosalyn had fallen under her spell like everyone else.

She knew there would be no punishment.

When Chloe returned to the house, there was an envelope without a stamp waiting for her on the hall table.

'A boy brought it,' said Mrs Foster.

Chloe recognised the handwriting on the front and, her heart beating faster, escaped with it to her bedroom where she tore it open and slid out the letter.

*I'll be in the summerhouse at half-past nine again tomorrow evening. Please try to come.'*

Chloe pressed her lips to the paper and slid it under her pillow.

'I couldn't wait any longer. I had to see you,' said Adam when she met him the following evening.

'Why?' She looked up at him teasingly from the shelter of his arms.

'To tell you that I love you.'

'You told me that yesterday.'

He bent his head and kissed her. 'And I shall tell you tomorrow and the next day and forever more.'

Her lips found his and her response was better than words.

They made themselves comfortable in the corner of the couch and he wrapped his arms round her more tightly.

She gazed round the shabby little summerhouse. 'I wonder how long it is since lovers met in here?' she mused. 'It doesn't look as if it's been used for years.'

'How long are we going to meet here?' He kissed the tip of her nose. 'When are you going to tell everyone about us?'

'In a little while. Everyone's wrapped up in Milly at the moment and I don't want to distract the family from that. I told Benedict the other evening because he was suspicious, but he promised to keep it to himself.'

She sat up and moved away from him.

'I must go back now. Mrs Keeling and Betty were listening to a play on the wireless. It should be over now and they'll wonder where I am.'

'Is Mrs Keeling quite better now?'

'Completely back to normal. Having Milly has helped so much.'

'I'll pop in and make sure on Monday morning.'

By then Betty had gone. She left late on Sunday afternoon with Benedict.

Milly waved sadly from the gate.

'She'll come back as soon as she can,' Chloe promised. 'Why don't you draw her a picture and we'll post it to her?'

Milly thought that was a good idea, and spent the next hour drawing a picture of Bubble and Squeak.

'Wasn't I clever to think of sending for Betty?' said Mrs Keeling with satisfaction. 'I wish we could find a way to keep her here.'

In the not-too-distant future there might be an excellent way, Chloe mused, but that thought wasn't for sharing just yet.

She and Milly set off for a walk the next morning before Adam had paid his visit to Mrs Keeling. Milly clutched the envelope containing the picture for Betty.

At the shops, they posted the picture and then bought some muffins for tea.

'Muffins! What a funny word. Muffins. Muffins.' Milly's smile was gleeful. 'Shall we take some muffins for Papa, too?'

'We'll take enough for everyone,' said Chloe. 'You can sit on the rug in front of the fire with Grandmother, and toast them with a long fork. Then we'll put lots of butter on them. They're very good.'

Chattering happily, they soon found themselves back at Hampdens and, to Chloe's delight, she saw Adam's car parked at the gate. He must have waited for her.

'Go in to Grandmother,' she said to the child. 'I'll be in very soon. I just want to speak to the doctor.'

She turned to the car with a happy smile, which faded abruptly when she saw the expression on Adam's face.

'Is anything wrong?'

'I don't like being taken for a fool.' He spoke quietly but his tone was furious.

'But ... but ... ' What was he talking about? She was too stunned to get out the words.

'You told me there was nothing between you and Benedict. You said he was interested in Betty. What were you doing? Trying to punish me? No wonder you didn't want to tell everyone about us.'

'I don't know what you mean. Why are you talking like this?'

'I've just been with Mrs Keeling. She told me that you and Benedict are to be married!'

As she stared in bewilderment, his car roared off down the lane.

# A Wedding At Last!

Shocked, Chloe stood motionless until the tail end of the car had disappeared. She and Benedict were to be married? She hurried into the house — Mrs Keeling was the key to this confusion.

The old lady was sitting in an armchair by the fire with her feet on a footstool, embroidering Milly's name on to a handkerchief. The child stood next to her, watching carefully. They both looked up as Chloe rushed in.

'There you are, Chloe. Oh, my goodness, my dear, is anything wrong?'

'What did you say to Adam?' Chloe burst out.

Mrs Keeling blinked. 'Adam? You mean Dr Raven? Why? What has he said?'

Milly was looking from one to the other, sensing that something was wrong.

Chloe took her to the door and gently shooed her out. 'Go to the kitchen and ask Mrs Foster for a biscuit and a drink,' she said, and returned to Mrs Keeling.

The old lady set aside her embroidery. 'I can see you're very upset about something. Come and sit down.'

Chloe collapsed into the chair opposite, near to tears.

'Adam has rushed off in a fury. He said . . . he said . . . '

'Adam?' said Mrs Keeling wonderingly. 'You're on Christian names already?' She stared at Chloe, understanding dawning. 'Is it possible that the doctor is your long-lost love?'

Chloe nodded. 'He found out where I was, left his job and came to live in Cheston Parva. Dr Marchant needed a locum so . . . '

'I see.' Mrs Keeling looked thoughtful. 'So the story should have a happy ending. But you don't look happy.'

'He said you told him I'm going to marry Benedict.' Chloe looked up, her eyes brimming with tears. 'He didn't give me a chance to reply. He accused me of lying to him and just stormed off.'

Mrs Keeling leaned forward in her chair. 'He obviously misunderstood something I said. I most certainly didn't say you were going to marry Benedict. Now let me think . . . He was packing up his stethoscope and other bits and pieces and I was chatting away about Betty and Benedict. Perhaps I said they were going to be married — though that's wishful thinking on my part, I'm afraid. I'm very fond of Betty, as you know, and I want Benedict to have someone of his own. Dr Raven was probably only half listening; you know what men are — impatient with female ramblings! He heard 'Benedict' and 'married' and for some reason thought I meant to you.'

Chloe said nothing. She was thinking of the look on Adam's face.

'Shall I go and telephone him?' asked Mrs Keeling. 'After all, this is my fault.'

'No, it isn't,' said Chloe quickly. 'He shouldn't jump to conclusions like that. Why didn't he question you — or me, for that matter? He didn't give anyone a chance to explain, he just . . . reacted.' She sighed. 'I really don't know why I love him. He seems to cause me so many problems!'

'That's love,' said Mrs Keeling. 'Impossible to explain, impossible to resist. I'm sure that as soon as he calms down and thinks rationally, he'll be back and begging for your forgiveness.'

Chloe gave her a weak smile. 'I expect you're right. I'll just go upstairs and splash some cold water on my face. Then it'll be time for lunch.'

She picked up her coat, left the room and walked slowly and thoughtfully up the stairs.

How quickly happiness could vanish and misery take its place, she mused.

In her bedroom, she removed her hat and threw it on the bed. Then she moved dejectedly to the window and looked out. A car was coming up the lane. Could it be . . . ? It was! Adam!

She raced down the stairs and out of the door.

The car stopped abruptly at the gate and he flung himself out. He opened his arms as she ran towards him.

They clung together, unspeaking, until eventually he released her and looked down into her eyes.

'I'm a stupid, unthinking wretch,' he said. 'How could I believe that you and Benedict . . . ? After all we said to each other last night.'

'I'm not going to argue with you,' she said, with a tremulous smile.

'Oh, Chloe, my sweet little Chloe. Can you forgive me?'

'Only if you promise it will never happen again. That you will never assume something about me without making sure.'

'Perhaps if we spend more time together it won't happen again. In fact, if we spend all our time together, it can't happen again.'

'What do you mean?'

She tilted her head up to him and he gave her a gentle kiss.

'I mean I want to marry you. Will you, Chloe? Please?'

She wrapped her arms around his neck.

'I will. Of course I will.'

'Chloe.' He held her close. 'At last.'

They were standing in the shelter of a tall hedge, screened from the road, but Chloe suddenly realised that they were in full view of the house. She hoped everyone was in the dining-room at the back.

'You'd better come in and see Mrs Keeling,' she said. 'She feels dreadful because she thinks she's to blame for the mistake. I know she'll be happy to hear we've made up, and if she's concerned at losing me, I have a solution.'

★   ★   ★

'Married? Chloe, my dear, what wonderful news!' Mrs Keeling gave the girl a hug.

Then she turned to Adam.

'You gave us quite a fright,' she scolded.

'I know, and I'm sorry.'

'I was going to suggest that you have lunch with us,' she said, 'but perhaps you would like to take your fiancée out for a private meal.'

'I should like to stay here with you for lunch and take her out to dinner,' said Adam.

Mrs Keeling was delighted.

'Mrs Foster, lay an extra place for Dr Raven,' she said, 'and call Mr Benedict. We're going to have an engagement party.'

Adam, devastatingly handsome in a dinner jacket, called for Chloe at eight o'clock that evening.

'If I were fifty years younger, I'd try for him myself,' said Mrs Keeling with a twinkle in her eye.

At Adam's request, Chloe wore her ice-blue dress with the bow set low at the back. As they entered the dining-room of the hotel, his fingers played up and down her spine, and she found it hard to retain the dignity she felt the dress demanded.

'So that's why you wanted me to wear this dress,' she said, when they were seated.

'That's one reason. But I have another which you will discover in a moment.'

The waiter presented the menus and Chloe read hers with unseeing eyes.

'I'm so happy, I don't think I can eat anything,' she said.

'Well we can't just sit here! They expect us to order something,' he teased. 'Anyway, I'm happy, but I'm also hungry. Shall I choose for us?'

'No. I've decided. I shall have melon and raspberries to start with and then supreme of chicken.'

'Mm. A good choice. I shall have the same, but with lemon soup to start.'

'Lemon soup? Do you like that?'

'I don't know,' he said cheerfully. 'I've never tried it. But I feel like being adventurous tonight.'

'This is a sumptuous hotel,' she said, as they waited for their meal. 'I love the waitresses' Edwardian dresses and aprons.'

'I believe it was an Edwardian love nest. Appropriate, don't you think?'

'A love nest? Really? Whose?'

'Edward the Seventh's. He was keen on love nests. He bought this one for an actress friend. In fact, he bought several of them for actress friends. Then he could visit them in private.'

'So that's the reason for the Edwardian touches.'

Chloe studied the paintings of wasp-waisted ladies in ruffled dresses and huge hats.

The food matched the surroundings; old-fashioned but glamorous.

Chloe admired the arrangement of melon and raspberries on her plate and picked up her spoon.

'Have you told Betty our news?' asked Adam and she nodded.

'This evening. She was so pleased. She feels she arranged it all.'

'Well, if it hadn't been for her, I might have gone to America and we should never have met again.'

'Oh, Adam, I can't bear to even think about that!'

'Don't look so tragic. It didn't happen and nothing can separate us now.'

He reached into his jacket pocket and took out a small leather box.

'This will make quite sure.'

He opened the lid and Chloe gasped. On a velvet cushion nestled the most beautiful ring she could have imagined. It was designed like a flower, the centre a diamond, the petals small glistening sapphires.

'Now you know why I wanted you to wear your blue dress.'

He lifted the ring from the box and slipped it on to the third finger of her left hand. It fitted perfectly.

'Oh, it's beautiful,' she breathed. 'I don't know what to say. I think I want to cry.'

He raised one eyebrow. 'Please don't. The other diners will assume I've said something cruel to you,' he said in mock alarm.

He gestured to the wine waiter, a prearranged signal, and a few moments later they were toasting their future in sparkling champagne.

With the champagne came a dish of luscious looking chocolates. Chloe bit into one and discovered it was filled with thick, fresh cream.

Her eyes shone. 'Can we be greedy and eat them all?' she asked.

'I think that's the idea.'

'Oh, Adam, I'm so happy. This is a wonderful evening.'

He grasped her hands across the table, his green eyes shining.

'Could you bear some more excitement?'

'More excitement?'

'Have you thought what will happen when Dr Marchant returns to his practice?'

She looked puzzled. 'You'll find somewhere else to work, I suppose. Wherever it is, I shall be with you. We'll never be separated again.'

'What would you say if I told you that I'm going to set up my own practice?'

'That would be wonderful. But doesn't it take a great deal of money?'

'Yes, but I have enough — now. An elderly great-aunt whom I scarcely knew died a few months ago, and I heard last week that she very kindly left me her house. She didn't leave me any money but the house is large and in a desirable part of London. I'll be able to sell it for a good sum according to the solicitors.'

'So you really can set up your own practice?'

'Yes. And I shall save money on staff.'

'Because I shall be your nurse?'

'Exactly.' He leaned across the table. 'We'll make a wonderful team. Of course, in time you'll probably have other things to think about.'

Chloe blushed. 'I hope I shall.'

'Then I shall need to find another nurse.'

'I shall hire her,' said Chloe firmly. 'She'll be over forty and have very fat legs,' she declared, and Adam laughed.

She finished her champagne.

'It's right what they say — the bubbles do get up your nose.' She sighed. 'What a pity there is no dancing here.'

'It is a pity, but there's something equally romantic here. Something very

Edwardian, something different. Come on — . I'll show you.'

He led her from the dining-room, along a corridor and into an enormous conservatory. Globe lights shone among enormous potted palms, and here and there white wrought iron seats and little tables were tucked in among them.

'We can have coffee here,' said Adam. 'Let's find a secluded corner.'

When the coffee tray had been placed on the table in front of them and the waiter had gone, Adam took her hand. On the far side of the conservatory, a pianist began to play softly.

'I think I'm in heaven,' Chloe whispered as Adam pressed his lips to the soft palm of her hand.

Chloe decided to go and see Betty and Aunt Ellen before the old lady moved to Bournemouth.

'I shall be there by Christmas,' Aunt Ellen told her. 'It will be fun to have Christmas in a big hotel — all the guests and the decorations. I'm really looking forward to it.'

She beamed at the two girls. 'Of course, I feel sad that Betty is losing her home, but I've given her something to make up for it. She'll be able to buy a little flat of her own.'

She studied Chloe with her head on one side.

'You're looking very well,' she observed. 'Being an engaged young lady suits you. And to think you're going to marry that young doctor. You heard about Dr Blaine, I suppose?'

'I haven't had time to tell her yet,'

310

said Betty with a smile. No one but Aunt Ellen had been able to get a word into the conversation.

'Dr Blaine?' asked Chloe. 'Has something happened to him?'

'He's been made Mayor, as he wanted,' said Betty, 'and he's giving up the surgery. Dr Ramsden is taking over from him.'

'What about Susannah?' asked Chloe. 'Will she be Mayoress?'

'I think she will be — now,' said Betty. 'All that nonsense about the married man has been forgotten. We believe she's getting engaged to a very suitable young fellow.'

'I'm glad,' said Chloe, and meant it. 'I'm happy and I want everyone else to be happy. Even Dr Blaine and Susannah.'

'Anyway,' she went on, 'I didn't visit you to talk about Susannah Blaine and her father. Tomorrow we'll go and choose bridal wear.'

'Are we having the dresses made?'

'No. We're going to the new shop at

the end of the High Street. They sell nothing but wedding dresses and bridesmaids' dresses. I want us both to look amazing for Adam and Benedict.'

Betty laughed delightedly. 'It will be like old times to go shopping together!'

Six weeks later, Chloe and Adam were married at the little village church in Cheston Parva. Mrs Keeling had begged them to marry from her house. Chloe's brother and sister-in-law had agreed and were happy to be there as guests.

The week before had been mostly rainy, but the wedding day dawned dry and a weak sun shone from a pale, wintry sky.

Chloe was a beautiful bride. Her white silk dress hung in a column from her shoulders. Her veil of rich lace was draped across her hair and secured by a circlet of white and silver flowers.

'She looks like a beautiful marble statue,' said Mrs Foster.

Benedict had discovered another facet to Rosalyn — she was a keen photographer. As such she was engaged to take the wedding photographs and proudly marshalled the guests into artistically arranged groups.

Betty, in a long white dress decorated with silver ribbons, was chief bridesmaid. She was happy to stand with Dr Ramsden, the best man, for the photographs, but Chloe was amused to see how quickly she and Benedict gravitated towards each other afterwards.

'How long will it be before we have another wedding, do you think?' asked Mrs Keeling, chatting to Betty's Aunt Ellen. The two ladies had discovered a mutual interest in the new craze of cryptic crosswords.

'You must come and stay with me at the hotel in Bournemouth,' Aunt Ellen said to her new friend. 'When I'm settled, I'll write to you.'

Aunt Ellen's removal to Bournemouth had made possible Chloe's plan for Betty. Mrs Keeling was thrilled at the suggestion that Betty should take Chloe's place as her nurse-companion.

'If I'm to lose you then there's no-one I should prefer to take your place,' Mrs Keeling had said. 'And I know Benedict will be pleased.'

The winter sun added charm to the scene, but there was no warmth in it. Several guests were beginning to look very cold.

'I think we have enough group photographs now,' Adam said to Rosalyn, who, carried away by the importance of her role, would have remained clicking her camera all day. 'Let's go back to the house.'

Olivia appeared, holding a fairy-like Milly by the hand. The child wore a short, frilly white dress, white shoes and long white socks. She was swathed in a large, fluffy shawl to keep her warm. Olivia carried two shawls over her arm.

Benedict took one and wrapped it round a shivering Betty.

'I don't think these dresses were intended for a winter wedding,' she said, teeth chattering.

Adam wrapped the other shawl

around Chloe, careful not to disturb her dress. He pressed his lips to her cold cheek. 'How does it feel to be Mrs Adam Raven?'

'You can't imagine,' she said. 'It's quite wonderful.'

At the house, the guests were warmed with goblets of hot punch.

Mrs Foster, with the help of a team of village women, had prepared a splendid wedding breakfast buffet. The table groaned under a feast of tiny sandwiches, colourful salads, cold meats, sparkling jellies and luscious cakes. In the centre towered the three-tiered wedding cake, glistening with white icing and decorated with tiny flowers.

'Mrs Foster has had a wonderful time preparing all this,' said Mrs Keeling. 'She hasn't had a chance to be so creative for years.'

Adam and Chloe moved among their guests, eating little, talking and laughing a lot. Now and then, as if by a secret signal, their eyes met and Chloe would feel her heart beating faster. Soon they would be alone and their life together would really begin.

When it was time to change into her going away outfit, she went upstairs with Betty. Her blue velvet coat-dress hung on the door of the wardrobe. Betty lifted it, stroking its silkiness, and held it out for Chloe to slip into. Then Chloe adjusted her little white fur hat and turned to her friend.

'How do I look? Fashionable enough for Paris?'

'Paris?' squeaked Betty. 'You're not going to Paris?'

Her face registered awe and envy.

'We are. Adam has just told me. He's been keeping it a secret. We're motoring down to the coast, staying at a hotel tonight and catching a boat to France in the morning. I have to pinch myself to see if I'm awake. Paris! I can't believe it.'

'Film stars go to Paris,' breathed Betty. 'And you'll look like a film star in that outfit. Wait till Adam sees you.'

Chloe caught Betty's hands. 'I'm so happy! I want you to be as happy as me. Soon it will be your wedding, I'm sure. I've seen the way Benedict looks at you. He loves you. And you love him, don't you?'

Betty looked down and blushed. 'Yes. And I know he loves me too because he's told me so himself. In fact . . . can you keep a secret? We're getting engaged at Christmas!'

Chloe flung her arms around her friend, pleased for Betty and Benedict, and also for Mrs Keeling. The old lady's dearest wish would come true.

'We must go down,' said Betty. 'Adam will be getting impatient.' She handed Chloe her bouquet and ran ahead of her to be part of the crowd.

Chloe paused at the top of the stairs. Faces smiled up at her and hands stretched high ready to catch the bouquet. She tossed it towards the group and laughed happily to see Betty's face glowing triumphantly above the flowers.

Adam reached and took her hand. Then he led her down the stairs through the crowd of friends and relations, his face shining with pride.

'Mrs Raven and I,' he began, to shouts and whistles of approval, 'will look forward to seeing you all when we return from Paris.'

More shouts and a round of applause.

The crowd parted and the happy couple made their way out to their car where Mrs Keeling was waiting to hug and kiss them both.

'When you return it will be only a few weeks to Christmas,' she said. 'I shall expect you to spend it here with us. We'll have a wonderful family party. Goodbye, my darlings. Enjoy yourselves.'

Chloe turned and looked through the small back window as they drove off. She could just see Mrs Keeling and Olivia waving, and Milly jumping up and down between Betty and Benedict. Rosalyn was pointing her camera in the hope of getting a last photograph.

A year ago, Chloe had known none of these people, except Betty, but now they were like a family to her. And next to her was the most precious person of all; her beloved Adam. At last he belonged to her and she would never let him go. He turned and smiled.

'Happy, darling?'

She rested her head on his shoulder. 'Oh, yes!' she said.

## THE END

*Other titles in the*
*Linford Romance Library:*

## SEASONS OF CHANGE

**Margaret McDonagh**

When Kathleen Fitzgerald left Ireland twenty years ago, she never planned to return. In England she married firefighter Daniel Jackson and settled down to raise their family. However, when Dan is injured in the line of duty, events have a ripple effect, bringing challenges and new directions to the lives of Dan, Kathleen and their children, as well as Kathleen's parents and her brother, Stephen. How will the members of this extended family cope with their season of change?